9

A DIXIE MORRIS ANIMAL ADVENTURE

GILBERT MORRIS

MOODY PRESS

CHICAGO

P9-DTL-490

ISBN: 0-8024-3371-5

1 3 5 7 9 10 8 6 4 2

Printed in the United States of America

To my two best friends—
Amanda Parker and Rachel Pegoda.
I love you guys. Yeah, let's go, Saints!
Dixie

CONTENTS

1
BIG NEWS

Nothing in the world was much more fun to Dixie Morris than a wedding.

As she studied herself in the dressing room mirror, she had to admit that riding the barrels in a rodeo might be more *exciting*. Still, when it was your pretty aunt getting married and you were the maid of honor, that was exciting stuff.

Slowly Dixie turned around, critically examining herself and the dress she wore. She was almost twelve and perhaps more conscious of clothes than most girls her age. The dress was made of tea-length light pink satin and taffeta. It had a sweetheart neckline edged with white lace, short puffy sleeves, and a pink sash around the waist decorated with pink and white roses.

Then Dixie smoothed her long blonde

hair. She was glad that she had not taken Jared's advice to cut it short. Short hair would be easy to take care of, she admitted. But she thought long hair was worth the trouble. It was her best feature. She studied her face and found it just barely satisfactory. She had large blue eyes and an oval face and a nose that turned up ever so slightly, which she did not like.

Satisfied with her inspection, she left the dressing room and went to find Jared Eagle. *In a way,* she thought, *Jared and I are going to be like brother and sister. At least, maybe cousins.*

Jared's father, James Eagle, was marrying Dixie's aunt, Sarah Logan. It had been a whirlwind romance. James was half Sioux Indian and had two children—Jared, eleven, and Dreama, eleven months. James's first wife had died when Dreama was born.

The gossips of the town had guessed that Sarah, attractive and one of the best veterinarians in the state, would never agree to marry him. But she had, and now the big day had arrived!

Dixie found Jared ushering people into the auditorium. The church was already filling up.

"Who's taking care of Dreama?" she asked.

"Your uncle and aunt." Jared was a lanky boy. He had the blackest possible hair, dark blue eyes, and bronze skin. Right now he pulled at his white collar as though it was choking him.

"What's the matter with you?"

"I hate wearing this suit, and I hate weddings!"

"You look very handsome—and I *love* weddings!"

"Well, that's you, and this is me!" Jared grumbled. He kept tugging at the collar until Dixie reached up and slapped his hand.

"Stop that!" she demanded. "This is one of the happiest days in your dad's life!"

Jared had the grace to look ashamed. "I know it, and I'm glad, too."

"You ought to be! Now you'll have a mom, and Dreama will grow up with a mom. So why don't you smile and look happy?"

Jared shoved up the corners of his mouth with his forefingers and managed to look absolutely ridiculous. Then he scowled. "I just hate to get dressed up. What about after Dad and Mom go off on their honey-moon, you and I go fishing?"

"Sounds like a winner to me." Dixie peered into the auditorium, "The church is almost full!"

"I hope Dad doesn't faint." Jared grinned. "He was pretty nervous this morning."

"So was Aunt Sarah."

"Are you?"

"Oh, no. I just have to stand beside Aunt Sarah while she's getting married. I'm the maid of honor—the main one. The way we're doing it at this wedding, I go in first."

"You always have to be number one," Jared said. "Be sure you don't mess things up. My dad doesn't get married every day, you know."

"Mess things up! I've practiced walking down that aisle for two weeks. I could do it backwards with my eyes closed. I've got to go now, but you just watch when I come marching in."

And then time seemed to shoot by like a bullet. After nervously checking her hair and her dress again, Dixie joined the other bridesmaids, Mary Prince and Eileen Dort-meyer. Mary was her aunt's best friend from school days. Eileen was another close friend. Aunt Sarah had once saved her dachshund's life.

"There's the music," Eileen said. "Are you ready, Dixie?"

Taking a deep breath, she nodded. "All ready."

Dixie stepped out into the foyer and began her trek toward the front. According to plan, she would go in, then Mary, then Eileen. The pastor would come in at the front with Mr. Eagle and his three attendants. And then the bride would come down the aisle.

Dixie had diligently practiced. She was determined not just to walk as if she were strolling along the street. She had practiced how to take a step forward, then bring up her other foot and pause briefly, then step ahead.

She concentrated intently on keeping her rhythm right, but at the same time her eyes were looking everywhere. Uncle Roy was turned all the way around, watching her come. His red face was beaming. And Aunt Edith, thin and nervous and wearing a new pink dress, was smiling encouragement.

She passed by Sheriff Peck and by her good friend Candy Sweet, tall and strong, the handyman for her uncle and aunt on the farm. He grinned at her.

Dixie was so involved in keeping the rhythm and in looking at people that she did not notice the narrow grill in the center of the aisle in front of her. It was part of the air conditioning system and was almost unnoticeable, being set down into the thick carpet.

Dixie had been very proud to be wearing new high-heeled shoes, but suddenly she was aware that one heel had slipped into the grill in the floor! Frantically, she tried to jerk it loose, but it was stuck.

Her mind had never worked so fast! *I can't stop and make a spectacle out of myself trying to get this shoe out!* she thought. In a flash of inspiration, she simply took her foot out of the shoe. Without missing a beat, Dixie took the next step and the next. She was very pleased with herself. Most people wouldn't be able to see that she was half barefooted.

She learned later what happened next.

Behind her, Mary Prince saw the shoe. She did not miss a beat, either. When she got to the grill, right in time with the music she stooped over and picked up the shoe, thinking she could give it to Dixie.

The problem was that, instead of picking up just the shoe, it was stuck so firmly that the grill came with it, leaving a gaping hole in the floor.

Eileen Dortmeyer was right in time with the music also. She did not even notice Mary stooping over, and she did not see the hole in the floor. She stepped right into it.

A piercing cry broke out in the church. Dixie could not help turning around and staring—as did everyone else. There was Eileen Dortmeyer in a very strange position. Then she realized that Eileen was up to her knees in the air conditioning return.

Everything had to stop, even the organ music, in order to get Eileen out. Candy Sweet finally got up and put his hands under Eileen's elbows and just lifted her out.

Dixie wanted to fall through the floor herself, but Mary Prince just said in a loud, clear voice, "I think we'd better try this one more time."

They started over, and the second entrance went smoothly. But Dixie was sure that for the rest of her life she would blush when she remembered Aunt Sarah's wedding to James Eagle.

After the ceremony, when everyone was in the reception room, a laughing Aunt Sarah put her arms around Dixie. "I'd give anything if I could've been in there to see the fun!"

Mr. Eagle, tall and looking very handsome in his tuxedo, was grinning, too. "It must have taken you a long time to think up a stunt like that, Dixie."

In fact, everyone teased her. But just before the new couple left for their wedding trip, they both hugged her again, and Sarah whispered, "Don't you worry about what happened, honey. It wasn't your fault. Things turned out just fine."

And her new husband whispered, "I'm just as married as if you hadn't set off a little bomb for us." Then Mr. Eagle said, "When we get back, you and I will have to go bird hunting."

So off they went, the bride and groom, and Dixie Morris stood watching them go.

Jared was standing beside her. He said, "I guess we're on our own for a while."

"I guess so." Dixie had been happy for Aunt Sarah and still was. But somehow she knew that something had changed and that things could not again be exactly what they had been.

Jared and Dreama stayed at Uncle Roy and Aunt Edith's during the honeymoon. One afternoon, Dixie was playing Monopoly with Jared on the living-room floor. She was winning, and Jared was taking his loss badly.

He picked up a card and stared at it. "Go to jail!" he exclaimed. "That's all I do in this dumb game—go to jail!"

"You have to pay fifty dollars to get out," Dixie reminded him with a grin.

But the two loved to play Monopoly, and it was usually a noisy game. Both of them would shout and complain. Today, however, Dixie's mind was not on the game.

After a time, Jared seemed to sense that. "What's the matter with you?" he asked. "I landed on Boardwalk, and you've got a hotel there, and you didn't even notice!"

"Oh, I guess I'm just—I don't know." Dixie shrugged.

"I bet I know. You miss your mom and dad."

Dixie looked up. Jared was very perceptive. "I do. They've been gone for a year, and it's been great staying here, and I had a good time in the circus with Aunt Sarah. But it's not the same as being with your own family."

The game ended soon after that, and they went fishing for a while. When they came back, Jared cleaned the fish, and then Dixie helped Aunt Edith cook them.

While Dixie was setting the table, the telephone rang. Her aunt picked up the phone and then said excitedly, "Dixie, it's for you—it's Africa!"

Dixie almost dropped a plate. She ran straight to the phone and cried, "Hello?"

Her mother's voice came over the wire, saying, "Dixie, we've got good news for you!"

Dixie's heart leaped. "Did you get the house finished?"

"Almost. It'll be finished in three months."

"And I can come and be with you?"

"Yes!"

"Hooray!" Dixie shouted, as everyone gathered around her. "I'm going to Africa!" she told them. Then she said, "When can I come, Mom?"

"We want you to fly with a young lady who's going to be a missionary here. Her name is Clarissa Harlow. She and her mother will take care of you for the next three months—then you can come out with her."

"Where does she live?"

"In Alaska."

"I'm going to Alaska!" Dixie announced to Jared and her uncle and aunt and Candy.

After she hung up, Dixie tried to answer their questions.

Right away, Aunt Edith got teary eyed. "We're going to miss you, Dixie," she said.

"We sure will," Uncle Roy said. "Don't know what we'll do without you around here."

"I'll miss you, too. A lot."

Candy Sweet was silent.

She took his big hand in hers. "And I'm going to miss you, Candy. You've been one of my best friends ever since I came here."

Candy Sweet looked sad. But he also looked at Dixie fondly, and he shrugged his big shoulders. "You'll be with your mom and dad, and that's what counts."

2
A BIT OF HELP

Dixie clung to her uncle, kissed him, and then whispered in his ear, "I'll write you all the time, Uncle Roy."

Aunt Edith was waiting. She had cried twice on the way to the airport, but now she had better control of herself. Working up a smile, she said, "You're the sweetest girl in the world, Dixie. Don't forget your Uncle Roy and Aunt Edith."

Throwing her arms around her aunt, Dixie hugged her tightly and was close to tears herself. "I won't. You've been better to me than anybody!"

Then a blue-uniformed woman came along and said, "You'd better get on board. You wouldn't want to get left behind."

Dixie gripped her carry-on case and turned toward the door that led to the big jet. She paused only once for a last look at her uncle and aunt. They waved. She waved back, a lump in her throat. Then she wheeled and almost ran down the long corridor to the plane.

When Dixie got to the door of the aircraft, a smiling blonde flight attendant met her. "Are you traveling all alone, miss?"

"Yes, ma'am. I'm going all the way to Alaska by myself."

The flight attendant took Dixie's boarding pass. "I'll show you your seat and help you store your suitcase."

Dixie followed the girl down the length of the plane. Almost every seat was filled.

"Here we are," the attendant said. "Twenty-six A. Right by the window. You can see everything—all the way to Alaska."

"Thank you," Dixie said.

And then the girl offered to store away her small carry-on case. As soon as we're in the air, she said, "I'm going to bring you a nice lunch. If you want anything, just push that button right overhead."

"Thank you."

Dixie waited until the two people in the outer seats stood and let her in. Then she plumped down by the window and fastened her seat belt. She had flown before and knew what to do.

"You're going all the way to Alaska, are you?" The speaker was the lady beside her, an elderly woman with a friendly smile.

"Yes, but I won't be there long. I'll only be there three months, and then I'm going to Africa."

"You *are* a world traveler. Tell me why you're going to Africa."

"Well, my parents are missionaries there. They went last year, but there was no place for me to live until they got a house built. So I've been with my uncle and aunt. Now I'm going to stay with another missionary, and she's going to Africa, too—to work with my mom and dad."

"That's interesting!" Then the woman laughed. "I hadn't even gone out of my hometown when I was your age. And here you are, going to Alaska and Africa."

Dixie loved to fly. As the plane took off, it gave her a thrill to see the ground fall away. She watched the cars grow smaller and smaller, and when the plane reached 30,000 feet, they were so tiny she could hardly see them. She enjoyed watching the landscape below until the flight attendant came with lunch.

"I hope you like breast of chicken and strawberries."

"Yes!" Dixie pulled down the little tray in front of her. Then she eagerly ate her lunch. When the lady beside her didn't eat her strawberries, she offered them to Dixie. Dixie ate them as well, then went back to looking out the window.

I'll see my mom and dad in only three months! She wondered briefly about the people she would be staying with in Alaska, but then she grew drowsy. Her last thought was: *I can stand anything for three months, no matter how bad they are.*

When Dixie got off the plane in Alaska, a blast of cold air bit into her. She had worn only medium-weight clothes, and now wished she had on something much heavier. She walked into the waiting room and looked around quickly. She had no idea what Clarissa Harlow looked like.

And then she heard a voice saying, "Dixie? Over here!"

Turning around, Dixie saw a young lady coming toward her. She wore wool slacks and a heavy black-and-white-checkered Mackinaw. She had a stocking cap on her blonde hair and looked very much like an outdoor person.

"I'm Clarissa Harlow, and I'll bet you're Dixie."

"Yes, ma'am."

"You can just call me Clarissa. We don't stand on ceremony out here in the backwoods. Let's pick up your luggage."

Clarissa peppered Dixie with questions while they collected her bags. It was quite a collection, too. She was carrying everything she wanted to take to Africa, except for her collection of Barbie dolls, which Uncle Roy had promised to ship later.

Then they walked out of the terminal, and once again the chilly air bit into her.

"Here we are. Right over here." Clarissa led the way to a white Land Rover and stored the baggage briskly. "I bet this weather is cold for you!"

"It sure is. I wonder what the temperature is."

"It was fifteen below last night. We have twelve inches of snow, and it looks like there's more coming. We'd better hurry if we don't want to get caught out in it."

Shivering, Dixie got into the vehicle.

When Clarissa Harlow climbed in, she said, "We'll get this heater going. Coming all the way from the South to the northern part of Alaska is quite a shock to the system."

She started the engine, and by the time they had cleared the airport and were on their way, Dixie was growing more comfortable.

Looking out the window, she could see nothing but a sheet of white. From time to time, there were rolling hills, broken by timber, but mostly the countryside was flat.

"I thought Alaska was full of *mountains*," she said. "Like the Rockies."

"Oh, we've got lots of mountains, but not here. We're kind of like the eastern part of Colorado, where they grow all the wheat."

Dixie sat watching the snow come down and answering the questions that Clarissa kept asking. It was snowing harder now, she realized, and seeing the road ahead was quite difficult.

"Aren't you afraid to drive in snowstorms?"

Clarissa laughed. "If I were, I'd never go anywhere. We have a lot of snow around here. And more this year than is usual." A small worry line appeared on her forehead. "For a fact, I hope we make good time this afternoon. I'd hate to get caught out in this if it worsens."

Looking out at the white world where powerful gusts of wind sent the snow swirling, Dixie shivered but not from cold. "Were you ever caught out in a storm?"

"Just once, and I vowed I'd never get into a situation like that again."

"Maybe we ought to turn around and go back?"

"Too late for that," Clarissa said. "We're past the point of no return."

"What does that mean?" Dixie asked. "It sounds bad."

"I meant it's as far to go back as it is to go on to Bannock."

"Is that the name of the town where you live?"

"That's right."

"Have you been there all your life?"

"Yes, I have. I was born there."

"Is it a big place?"

"Very small. You'll probably be bored to death."

"No, I won't. It was a small town where I was."

"We're cut off from the rest of the world for part of the year. This part particularly. But we have fun. We go skiing and sledding and snowshoeing—all kinds of winter things."

That sounded like fun to Dixie, so she settled back and watched the scenery. They drove for two hours, and all the time the snow on the road was getting deeper. Several times the vehicle almost slid off, and Dixie's heart came into her throat.

Clarissa said, "It won't be long now, Dixie. We're almost there."

But even as she spoke, suddenly there was a loud banging. The engine started to run roughly, and they began to slow down.

"What's the matter with this thing!" Clarissa muttered. She tried pumping the gas pedal. But abruptly the engine died, and the vehicle came to a complete stop.

All was still.

Dixie looked around. The snow was coming down so hard she could hardly see twenty feet away. Quickly she looked back to Clarissa. "Won't it start again?"

"I hope so," Clarissa said grimly.

She tried the engine several times, but it wouldn't start.

"I'd better get out and see if I can tell what's wrong," she said.

Dixie felt fear creeping over her.

The wind was howling like a wounded animal as Clarissa, with a flashlight, peered at the engine. Then she slammed down the hood and quickly got back in. Her face was grim. "I don't know what the problem is. I'm not very good with engines."

"What do we do?"

"We'll have to wait until this storm stops. Then we'll hike into town."

"How far is that?"

"About four miles. But maybe some-body will come along." She looked out at the whirling snow. "People don't travel much in these storms, though." Then she glanced at Dixie. "It's going to get real cold in here without the heater. We're pretty well fixed—I always carry blankets. And we have a Thermos of hot chocolate. But you need to put on all the clothes you can."

They opened a suitcase, and Dixie strug-gled into the warmest clothing she could find, including two sweatshirts and a heavy bomber jacket that had belonged to her father. She also pulled on three pairs of socks and then shoved her feet into some loose-fitting boots.

"That ought to do for a while, but the temperature's dropping—fast."

The howling wind rocked the vehicle, as if with a giant hand. Both Dixie and Clarissa tensely watched out the windows. No other car came along. Time seemed to crawl.

Finally Dixie asked, "How long have we been here?"

Clarissa glanced at her watch. "Three hours. It'll be dark soon. I guess we might as well figure on staying the night. We have the rest of the hot chocolate. You want some right now?"

"Should we save it till later?" Then Dixie cried, "Look out there! What's that?"

Clarissa squinted into the snowstorm. Then she let out a glad yip. "It's a dog team and sled! We're OK, Dixie!"

Shoving the door open, Clarissa yelled as she got out. "Here! Over here!" The snow was now well above her knees.

Then Dixie saw a team of huskies materialize out of the storm. She heard the driver yell, "Whoa!" and the dogs stopped.

Dixie got out, too. A man was walking

toward them. He was tall and wore a hooded jacket and thick gloves.

"Lars Bjoren, am I glad to see you!"

The big man stopped, shaking his head. "You don't have any business out in a storm like this."

"I know it. The car just quit on me. Can you go get some help for us?"

"Temperature's dropping. It's thirty below already." He looked at the two of them. "Get in the sled."

"Do you think the dogs can pull us all?"

"Just get in the sled! Quick!"

"All right. Come along, Dixie!"

Dixie had trouble walking through the deep snow. She passed by the lead dog, who gave her a look but did not move. She wondered if he didn't like people. She passed by four other dogs in double teams.

By the time they got back to the sled, the big man was throwing out supplies to make room for them. When there was space, he said gruffly, "Get in. Both of you."

"Come on, Dixie." Clarissa climbed in. "Sit in my lap here."

Almost numb with the cold, Dixie settled down in front of Clarissa, as Mr. Bjoren disappeared somewhere behind them.

Then he called out, "Go!" and at once the dogs started. She watched all their fluffy tails wag, and she heard the man's feet. He was following along at a trot.

Dixie had never had a ride like this! She had ridden a tiger when she was with the circus, but this was different. The snow was still coming down. All five dog tails stood up in plumes. From time to time one of the huskies would bark shrilly. When Mr. Bjoren called out, "Gee!" the team would veer to the right. When he shouted, "Haw!" they would go left.

"I never saw anything like this, Clarissa."

"Lars Bjoren is about the best man with dogs in this country, and this is a fine team. Look how they pull."

The sled moved almost silently over the snow. From time to time, Lars Bjoren would walk ahead and break trail for the dogs. The lead dog would follow him, keeping back about ten feet.

"That's a smart lead dog," Clarissa told her. "He knows just what his master is doing." And then she said, "Look, Dixie. There are the lights of Bannock."

Soon the dogs were plowing down what seemed to be the main street. It was wider than most streets and was lined with rows of buildings, all now covered with snow. Lights shone out of the windows, making them look yellow.

Soon Mr. Bjoren pulled up the dog team in front of a store.

"This is where I live," Clarissa said. "Above the store."

Clarissa got out, but when Dixie tried to follow her, she found that she could not move her legs. "I'm numb!" she said.

Mr. Bjoren came and picked her up easily, set her on her feet, and held her upright, saying, "Stamp your feet, girl."

Finally Dixie's feet began to tingle. She said, "Thank you so much. I don't know what we would have done if you hadn't come along, Mr. Bjoren."

The big man didn't respond. He just walked back to the sled, called out, "Go!" and the team moved away.

"I didn't even get a chance to properly thank him," Clarissa said.

"Where does he live?"

"Just on the outside of town. Not too far. Let's get inside. You need to thaw out."

Inside the store, an older woman greeted

them warmly. "This is my mother, Mrs. Harlow," Clarissa said.

"Where's the Land Rover?" her mother asked, but then she said to Dixie, "What a welcome to Alaska! Well, I've got hot soup and a good fire."

Soon Dixie was sitting at a table upstairs, spooning down soup, and listening to Clarissa tell the story of their adventure. "We'll have to get the Land Rover towed in to the repair shop tomorrow," she said.

When she was through, Dixie asked, "Why didn't Mr. Bjoren stay and come in?"

A look passed between the two women. Mrs. Harlow said, rather mysteriously, "He wouldn't come into this place under any conditions."

Dixie glanced at her face and realized that something was wrong. She didn't know what it was, but she thought, *They don't like each other—Mr. Bjoren and Mrs. Harlow. I wonder why. I'll have to find out.*

3
AN OLD STORY

Dixie did not sleep well her first night at the Harlows'. Her room seemed to creak and groan and shake all night long with the wind that howled around the building.

When daylight began to send gray light through her window, she got up. The room was cold. Shivering, she quickly pulled on the thermal underwear that Aunt Sarah had bought for her stay in Alaska, along with two pairs of socks, wool pants, and a heavy blue sweater.

When she went out into the living area, the heat from a huge stove was pleasant indeed. She found her way to the kitchen, where Clarissa was already making breakfast.

"You're up early, Dixie!"

"I woke up earlier than usual. Can I help you fix breakfast? I like to cook. I know how to make scrambled eggs."

"Sure. You can start the eggs while I do the biscuits. My mother had some work to do outside. She'll be in later."

The stove was an old wood burner, a massive thing such as Dixie had never seen. It threw out waves of welcome heat, but Dixie discovered that using it was a little different from cooking with electricity.

"Why don't you have an electric stove?"

Clarissa shrugged. "Oh, Mom's had this stove ever since she got married. She doesn't like to change her ways."

The kitchen was soon full of the savory odors of bacon frying and coffee bubbling in the percolator and biscuits baking. By the time the two sat down, Dixie was ready to eat.

"Why don't you ask the blessing, Dixie?"

Dixie bowed her head. "Lord, we thank You for my safe trip and for this food. Bless this house. In the name of Jesus. Amen."

"Plunge in. There's plenty more where this came from," Clarissa said cheerfully.

The biscuits that Clarissa had made were large and fluffy and good. As Dixie spread butter on one after another, she said, "We were lucky to get out of that mess we were in yesterday. Weren't we, Clarissa?"

"Not lucky. The Lord was looking after us. It would have been pretty cold out there all night with no heat. Especially for a new-comer."

Dixie chewed on a bite of biscuit and strawberry jam. "What did you say the man's name was that rescued us?"

"Lars Bjoren."

"He didn't stay long, did he? I thought he might come in." Dixie had not forgotten how strangely the two women had behaved when talking about Lars Bjoren.

Clarissa stirred a spoonful of sugar into her coffee. She obviously had something on her mind. At last she said, "There's a long story behind that, Dixie."

"What kind of a story?"

For a moment it seemed as though Clarissa would not answer. Then she said, "Well, you might as well hear it from me. You will anyhow. Years ago, Lars Bjoren dated my mother."

"He did? You mean before she married your father?"

"Well, of course! They were both dating her. My father and Lars Bjoren. They were all young then."

Dixie opened another biscuit, buttered it, then tried the blackberry jam. It was as good as the strawberry. "That must be kind of peculiar—to have a fellow around who used to date your mother."

"As I said, it all happened a long time ago." She took another sip of coffee. "Lars took it hard when Mother chose Dad instead of him."

"You mean it broke his heart?" Dixie thought that sounded romantic.

"Something like that. He didn't stay around Bannock long. He moved away and came back only a few years ago."

"Did he ever get married?"

"Never did. He made a lot of money, though. He was in construction work all over the world. Came back here and bought a place just on the edge of town. But he's really turned into a hermit." She sighed. "It's sad. He stays out in that big house all alone and raises sled dogs. I will say this for him, he's about the best dog trainer in Alaska."

"You mean like those dogs that pulled us last night?"

"Yes. Siberian huskies. People come

from all over the world to buy his dogs. He's very particular, too. He won't sell them to just anyone who has the money."

Dixie considered another biscuit, then patted her stomach. "I'd better not eat another one. Well, that's too bad about Mr. Bjoren. I sure am glad he came along last night, though. I was praying God would send somebody."

"I was, too, but I never even thought about him and his sled dogs. He goes out in all kinds of weather. Nothing seems to bother him. He's got a plane too, and he just flies off sometimes. Nobody knows exactly where he goes."

Just then Mrs. Harlow came in, all warmly dressed. She was a very pretty older lady. She had light hair that she kept in braids that wound around her head. She patted Dixie on the shoulder. "Our new Alaskan. Did you save any biscuits for me?"

"Yes, ma'am, there's plenty left. They sure are good."

Mrs. Harlow sat down and began to eat and talk at the same time. She appeared to be a very outgoing woman and also very likable. Dixie was glad. *Otherwise,* she thought, *three whole months here might be hard to take.*

Later on, she helped Mrs. Harlow wash the dishes. "I bet you'll be sorry to see your daughter go to Africa. It's so far away."

A cloud crossed Mrs. Harlow's face. "It *will* be hard. But God's leading her that way, and I can't go against the Lord. But, yes, it's going to be very lonesome around here."

"Don't you have any relatives in Bannock?"

"No, Dixie. Not a one. Just Clarissa and me."

That seemed sad to Dixie.

Mrs. Harlow forced a smile. "But that's three months away. I learned a long time ago not to spoil a day by worrying about tomorrow. If we're healthy and have something to eat and a roof over our heads, let's thank the Lord for those things and rejoice and be glad." She began to tell stories of the Alaskan frontier as they finished the dishes. Then she said, "Why don't you come down to the store with me? You can help me there, or would you rather stay here?"

"Oh, no! I'd rather go. I'd like to meet some of the people around here."

"They'll be glad to meet you! Any newcomer in a village this small is a novelty. But let me warn you about Phineas."

"Who's Phineas?"

"Phineas Bean. He helps me in the store. He's an older fellow, and I don't know how I'd get along without him, but he's a regular prophet of gloom. He always sees the worst in everything. In any case, don't pay any attention to his gloomy predictions. Underneath, I think he's really cheerful."

Dixie found Phineas Bean to be exactly as Mrs. Harlow had described him. He was a small, lean man with a head of bushy salt-and-pepper hair. Bright brown eyes peered out at the world.

As soon as he met her, he said, "I'm glad to meet you, young lady. Of course, you come at a bad time of the year. Wouldn't doubt but what we have the worst blizzard of all times coming at us."

Dixie looked out the window. The sun was shining, and—though the snow was more than knee-deep—it seemed to be pretty weather. "It doesn't look so bad, Mr. Bean."

"That's the way these blizzards are."

Phineas Bean nodded vigorously. "Just like a woman—or a mule. They'll be good for a while to get you off your guard. Then they'll jump on you with all four feet."

Dixie grinned at his putting a woman and a mule in the same category. She said, "I think it'll be all right."

"That's right. That's right. Look on the bright side of it as long as you can," Phineas said. "Maybe I can show you around town this afternoon after I get some work done."

"I'd like that a lot!"

"Well, if we don't attacked by a wolf or a polar bear, maybe it'll be all right."

Dixie enjoyed working in the store. It was a huge, single room and was stacked with everything imaginable, including groceries, clothing, dog harness and equipment, bits and pieces of furniture, and pet medicines. It was like a museum. And there seemed to be little order in it all.

Phineas said, as they were putting cans on a high shelf, "One of these days the walls gonna push right out of this place. Mind what I tell you. Stuff in here is pushing the walls out, and down she'll go with a crash."

Dixie had already learned that when

Phineas complained, he did not mean much of what he said. She liked him very much.

Just before noon, a short woman with red hair laced with gray came in. She was also round like a sausage.

Phineas said quickly, "My dear, I'd like for you to meet Dixie Morris. Dixie, this is Mrs. Bean. Dorcas Bean, as a matter of fact."

Dorcas Bean's face was as round as the moon, and she obviously had some Eskimo blood. Her eyes were almost hidden in her face when she smiled. She greeted Dixie warmly. "I'm glad to meet you, Dixie. You must come and spend some time with us during your visit."

"That would be nice, Mrs. Bean."

Then Mrs. Bean turned on Phineas. "I thought I told you to get the wood chopped before you left home! You expect me to get out and chop it myself?"

"Well, my dear—"

But Mrs. Bean had no time for excuses. She proceeded to set forth a list of things that her husband had left undone.

And all the time his head was nodding up and down. He kept saying, "Yes, my love— indeed I forgot—true. Every word of it true."

After his wife left, Phineas said sadly, "A wonder of a woman—but she lies awake nights thinking of things I forgot to do."

"She's very nice. Do you have any children, Mr. Bean?"

"Five in all. All grown now and gone. Scattered all over Alaska. You'll be meeting some of them. They come back from time to time."

Three days after her arrival, Dixie went to church with Mrs. Harlow and Clarissa. And going to church was something she always liked to do.

The church building was only a small, one-room structure with a steeple on top. As they entered, Dixie saw Mr. Bean sitting up in the choir.

Clarissa said, "He can't sing much, but he does love to try."

They sat down close to the front, and the song service began. Dixie found that she knew most of the hymns that were sung. The song leader was a cadaverous-looking man with a booming voice. The pianist was Mrs. Bean. She attacked the piano as if it were something to be overcome.

Dixie hid a smile behind her hand and whispered to Clarissa, "She sure throws her all into it, doesn't she?"

"I remember what a visitor once said about her playing. He said she never missed a wrong note. But she does her best."

Actually, Dixie enjoyed the song service.

By now, the little building was packed. Clarissa whispered, "It's a good thing there are no fire wardens here. I think we are breaking all the fire laws ever written." Even the aisles were filled with chairs.

Then the preacher rose to speak, and everyone heaved a great sigh of anticipation.

"That's our pastor, Lewis Henderson," Mrs. Harlow whispered. "Fine man indeed!"

Mr. Henderson was a strongly built middle-aged man. He wore a brown suit with a white shirt and a blue tie. His eyes seemed to sparkle as he began to speak. "I see we have a visitor, Martha. Would you introduce her?"

Mrs. Harlow nodded at Clarissa, and Clarissa stood. "This is my young friend, Dixie Morris. Her parents are on the mission field in Africa where I'll be serving when I go. I want you all to be very nice to Dixie, because she's a fine young lady."

"Well, welcome to Bannock and to Alaska, Dixie," the pastor said, smiling warmly.

When Dixie shook hands with him as they left the church, he said, "Clarissa told me a little about your adventure. Kind of an exciting way to start a visit, wasn't it?"

"I was getting pretty scared. But we prayed, and then Mr. Bjoren came along with his dogs and his sled."

"Yes. Well, I thank the Lord that he did come along. I visit Mr. Bjoren regularly. Been doing that for five years. A good man."

"He's a Christian, then? I didn't know that."

"I believe he is. I think somehow he's gotten away from God—just wants to be alone. But the Lord never gives up on us, you know."

"Then I'll pray for him, Reverend."

Mr. Henderson's eyes smiled. "You do that! We'll pray together."

Dixie helped with dinner. She loved to cook, and she asked Mrs. Harlow to teach her how to make biscuits. She had made them before but never in a woodstove. She learned right away that Clarissa's mother didn't use a mix but started from scratch.

Martha started by measuring flour, baking powder, and salt into a large bowl. She cut the shortening into the dry ingredients until the mixture was crumbly, then added buttermilk. She stirred until all was moistened, sprinkled a dusting of flour onto the counter, put the dough mixture on it, and kneaded it a little. When she thought the dough was the right consistency, she rolled it out flat and cut out thick, round biscuits.

While the biscuit pan was in the oven, the two sat down. Dixie had a Dr. Pepper, while Martha had a cup of tea. She managed to get Mrs. Harlow talking about the old days. Finally she slipped it in: "You've known Mr. Bjoren a long time, haven't you?"

Martha looked straight at her and winked. "I guess you've been hearing all the stories. If it's possible for a girl to be in love with two men at the same time, I guess that was the time. Both such fine men. But I couldn't marry both of them."

"The pastor was saying that he thought Mr. Bjoren was a Christian," Dixie said.

"I believe he is, too. I've prayed for him ever since those days, and I'll never give up. He's made a hermit out of himself and missed out on a lot. But he's still a fine man."

Dixie saw that such talk saddened Mrs. Harlow. She thought, *I wish she could go to Africa with Clarissa. Maybe she could cook for the missionaries or something like that.*

Dixie Morris was always making plans for other people. Aunt Sarah had once told her, "Dixie, your spiritual gift is meddling!" Now once again, her mind was active, and her imagination flew as she thought about the months to come.

4

AN UNUSUAL VISITOR

Life in Alaska was an exciting new world. Dixie had seen a few snowfalls in the South but never any more than three or four inches deep. Here, sometimes the drifts against the hills or buildings were ten *feet* deep. She quickly learned to bundle up in thermals, and the air was so dry that— even though the temperatures were low—it was not bad at all.

The first week after Dixie's arrival, she stayed busy every day. She made friends quickly with a boy named Charles Bingley but whom everyone called Bingo. He was twelve. He had red hair and brown eyes. Another friend was Debby Sturgis, age ten, a spoiled brat who was fun when she got her own way.

Along with Bingo and Debby, Dixie

threw herself into having a good time. They laughed at her awkward attempts to walk with snowshoes. She would repeatedly step on the back of one snowshoe with the tip of the other and fall headlong. But falling into snow was not too bad.

The first day on snowshoes, she walked too far and the next morning cried out when she moved. Some of the muscles in the back of her legs had been overused, and she limped around. All that day they stayed inside Debby's house, playing games. That's when Dixie found that she had to let Debby win to keep her happy.

Later, they went sledding on the steepest hill in Bannock. The way it worked was, when you got to the top of the hill, you threw yourself down on your stomach on your sled and slid like lightning to the bottom.

Once, as Dixie was huffing back, tugging her sled, she said, "I wish they had lifts like they do at the ski areas."

"Me too," Bingo said. His cheeks were flushed. "No lifts around here. Just muscle power."

More than once Dixie lost control of her sled and went flying into the bushes—

which Bingo and Debby, both experts from a lifetime on skis and sleds and snowshoes, thought was wildly amusing.

One day, Dixie received a present from Mrs. Harlow—a pair of ice skates. She quickly discovered that because she had always skated a lot on roller blades, she could handle ice skates very well. Before long, she was sweeping along in long turns and skating backwards almost at full speed.

Dixie was at Bingo's house one Thursday. His father had gone to work, and his mother was busy in the kitchen. She and Bingo were sitting on the floor playing Parcheesi, and Bingo had just won a game, when suddenly they heard a cry from his mother.

"What's wrong, Mom?" he jumped up, and Dixie followed. They almost ran into Mrs. Bingley, coming out of the kitchen.

Her eyes were wide. "There's a polar bear at the back door!"

"I'll get the gun!" Bingo cried.

"No, just come in the bedroom and shut the door."

"Mom, those things can break a door down! Let me get the rifle." Bingo won the argument and ran off, soon to reappear with a large rifle in his hands.

"Now I hear him in the kitchen! Bingo, you let him alone unless he gets in here!" Mrs. Bingley said. "Even if you hit one of those big things, they can still grab you!"

Dixie was petrified. She had heard that polar bears could be a nuisance at times, but she never thought of one coming in the house.

The three of them listened, holding their breath, as noises from the kitchen indicated that the bear was indeed inside.

"Let me go out the front door and get the sheriff," Dixie said.

"No, you just stay here with us," Mrs. Bingley insisted.

Finally the noises ceased, and then Bingo let out a breath. "I think he's gone."

"Don't go into the kitchen yet," his mother warned.

But at that moment Dixie saw a magnificent, massive white polar bear wander past the window. He was licking his chops and had a contented look—for a polar bear.

"I'll bet he made a mess in the kitchen," Bingo said. He opened the door.

The three went into the kitchen, where Dixie saw that Bingo was right. The bear had pulled down everything he could get hold of. The room was a shambles.

"Oh, what a mess!" Mrs. Bingley groaned.

"I'll help you clean up, Mrs. Bingley," Dixie said.

She and Bingo both helped. Suddenly Dixie laughed out loud.

"What's so funny?" Bingo asked.

"Back home we might have a coon come stealing something, but we never had anything like a polar bear."

"They're migrating, I think," Bingo said. "They come through every year. They are real dangerous, but there's not much you can do about them."

That night, Dixie wrote in her journal about the polar bear incident and then excitedly wrote letters to her parents and to her uncle and aunt. She also wrote to Aunt Sarah and told her of her Alaska adventure.

After a few days, the snow had melted somewhat and formed a hard crust. Dixie went out walking and exploring and remembering Mrs. Harlow's words: "Don't stray too far away. You might run into one of those migrating bears."

The weather was warming up, and her cheeks felt rosy as she trudged along the streets. She was glad that her legs had lost their soreness from snowshoeing. Then she reached the outskirts of town. Here were stretches of forest. The country was more hilly and rocky toward the north, and Dixie took that direction just to see what it was like. She kept a sharp lookout but saw no bears. She did once see something that looked like a wolf, but she could not be sure. It ran immediately into some scrub timber.

She crossed a creek that was now thawed out and bubbling merrily along within its banks. She wondered if there were fish in it and decided to ask Bingo when she got back.

About a half mile from town she saw a house over to her right. It was low and rambling and appeared to be not very old. Then she could hear dogs barking. As she drew closer, a large dog appeared from behind a snowbank and blocked her way.

Dixie stood dead still, for the dog bared its long white fangs. "Nice dog," she said in a voice not quite steady.

The dog paid no attention to this and

took several paces forward, stiff-legged and with his head down.

Dixie was tempted to run, but she knew that would be useless. "Nice dog," she said in a firmer voice. But the dog took one more step toward her, and Dixie's heart sank.

"Rajah, beat it!"

Dixie looked up to see a tall man with blond hair and a short-clipped blond beard. She recognized him at once and let out a breath of relief. "Hello, Mr. Bjoren. Is that your dog?"

Lars Bjoren gave her a quick look. "You're the little girl that was caught out in the storm."

"Yes sir. Dixie Morris is my name."

"You shouldn't be wandering around out here," he said shortly. "There are bears on migration."

"I know. One of them came right into Bingo's house the other day."

"Be on your way home, then."

Dixie decided not to be put off by his gruffness. She said, "I want to thank you properly for what you did for Clarissa and me. If you hadn't come along, it might have been bad. I was getting pretty cold—and scared."

Lars Bjoren was handsome, she thought. He had the most brilliant, piercing blue eyes she had ever seen. He looked the way she imagined a Viking might have looked.

He started to turn away, and she said quickly, "Mrs. Harlow says you raise dogs."

"That's right." The answer was terse, and he began walking off.

"I wonder if you would mind showing them to me, Mr. Bjoren. I've never seen a Siberian husky up close. I've seen pictures, though. They're the most beautiful dogs I've ever seen."

He stopped and turned back toward her. "You've never seen a husky up close?"

"No sir."

"Then I don't suppose it would do any harm for you to look. This way."

Mr. Bjoren led Dixie around his house to where there were a number of wire pens, each with a small, individual doghouse inside. The dogs began to bark and rear up against the fences as they approached. He reached in and petted several of them, and they whined and licked his hand.

"This is a new one. I just got her. Haven't used her in harness yet." He opened a gate, and a dog came out. "You can pet her.

She's friendly. Too friendly for a sled dog, maybe."

Dixie put a hand on the husky's head, and the dog licked her hand. She had a deep chest, strong legs, and a powerful straight back. "Ooh, she looks so strong!"

"She weighs only about thirty-five pounds. Sometimes a good dog will go as high as seventy, though that's unusual."

"What's her name?"

"Missy."

Missy's coat was thick and soft. It was mostly dark brown, but around the foxlike face was a pale cream section that looked like a mask.

"She sure is beautiful. But what do you mean, she's too friendly to be a sled dog?"

"She could pull a sled, but she wouldn't make a good racing dog. She's been spoiled."

Dixie stroked the husky's head. "She's got one blue eye and one brown eye!"

"Not too unusual. And see here?" He dug his fingers into Missy's coat. "She's got an undercoat of fur right next to the skin. It keeps her warm in very cold weather."

Dixie petted Missy for a while. Then, as though the ice were broken, Mr. Bjoren took her from one pen to another, introducing her to all his dogs and telling her a little of their history. It seemed to Dixie that the man was lonely—as if he had not spoken to anyone for a long time and just wanted to talk.

She was truly interested in his dogs and said, "I've been around a lot of animals, but not around Siberian huskies." When he asked her what kind of animals, she said, "Oh, tigers . . . elephants . . ."

"How were you ever around tigers and elephants?" he asked in astonishment.

Dixie started telling him about her experiences when Aunt Sarah was a veterinarian with the circus.

He seemed to find that interesting. "Well, I never met a young lady who's ridden on a tiger."

"I've got pictures of me doing that," Dixie said. "I'll give you one, if you'd like."

Mr. Bjoren smiled for the first time. "Might like it a great deal. Would you care for some tea and cakes?"

Dixie immediately said, "I sure would. I've had a long walk."

He started to take her to the house.

But then Dixie saw a dog in a pen all by himself. "What's the matter with him?"

Lars Bjoren said, "That's Blizzard."

He sounded a little sad, and Dixie wondered what the trouble was.

"I got him when he was just a pup and have been training him. But I don't know if he'll ever make a lead dog. The lead dog I have now—Buck—he's getting old, and I was thinking I might try the Iditarod this year."

"What's that?"

"The Iditarod? The most famous dog race in the world! I've entered it three times but never have won. Think I have a chance with these dogs. But as I said, my lead dog is old. So I've been trying to train this one."

Blizzard did not get up. He was watching them, however, with alert blue eyes.

"What's wrong with him?"

"Right now he's hurt himself. But that's not the main problem. Every lead dog's got his own personality," Lars Bjoren said. "Some are stubborn, some are sly, some are just downright mean. I think Blizzard was mistreated before I got him, so he's still rebellious. But is that dog strong and smart! If he'd ever make up his mind just to work with me, I think we could win the Iditarod."

61

"Could I pet him?"

"No. He's snapped at me once or twice."

"I'm real good with animals. They all seem to like me."

"Well . . . as long as I hold onto him, it'll be all right." He undid the latch, and they entered the pen.

"Now, you behave, Blizzard!" he said. He knelt down and got a good hold on the husky, who growled deep in his throat.

Dixie knelt on the other side and began to croon, "Now, Blizzard, there's a nice dog. Nice dog." She kept on for some time, and the growling stopped. And then he turned and licked her hand!

"Well, I'll be—here I have to hold him to keep him from biting me, and he makes friends with you the first time! Sled dogs are like nothing else in this world. There's no explaining them."

Dixie petted Blizzard for a while longer.

"We'd better go in for that tea," Mr. Bjoren said.

She petted the husky one more time. "You be nice, Blizzard. I'd like to see you win that race."

Lars Bjoren shut the door and led the

way to the house. "You seem to be good with animals, Dixie," he said.

"They just seem to like me. I don't know why."

They went inside, and Dixie liked his house very much. She said so.

"It's new, isn't it?"

"I built it five years ago." He started making tea on an electric stove, and soon he brought out a cake. "I have to apologize for this. I'm not much of a cake maker. But it's the best I can do."

Dixie tasted the cake, and it really was not very good, but she was too nice to say so. "I know how to make cake. Maybe you could teach me about dogs, and I could teach you how to make gingerbread."

"You know how to make good gingerbread?"

Dixie's grinned. "Why, I'm the world's champion gingerbread maker! Tomorrow I'll bring the things from Mrs. Harlow's store and make you some."

Lars suddenly grew glum. He munched on the terrible cake, then shook his head. "She may not like your coming to visit me."

Dixie, knowing the story, felt sorry for the big man. "I don't think she'd mind. I'd have to tell her, though. I couldn't deceive her."

"Yeah. All right. Dogs and gingerbread. It's a deal," he said.

Dixie knew then how lonely he was— lonely enough that he would invite an eleven-year-old girl to come and visit.

When she got up to leave, she said, "I'll see you tomorrow, Mr. Bjoren, and maybe you can show me how to train dogs. Some-day, maybe, *I* could drive a team."

"You're mighty little for that, but if you can make good enough gingerbread, we'll give it a try."

Dixie looked back from the road and glimpsed Lars Bjoren standing out on the porch, motionless. She waved, and he lifted a hand in a parting gesture. Then he went back into the house.

"He sure is a lonesome man," she mur-mured as she made her way toward town. "It's a shame, too. He's real nice looking for an old man."

5

TRAINING BLIZZARD

Dixie sat on a kitchen stool, telling of her visit with Lars Bjoren. Mrs. Harlow listened as she moved about, putting supper together. Clarissa was minding the store.

A sad expression came over Mrs. Harlow's face. She put a pot on the old woodstove, then sat down on a stool across from Dixie. "He was such a good man, Dixie. And always full of fun," she said.

"He seems so lonesome. Doesn't he have any friends?"

"No, and he could have lots of friends, but he stays out there in that house all the time, alone except for his animals."

"Doesn't he ever come to church?"

Martha shook her head. "When we were young, it was nothing to get into a truck and drive all the way over to Bennett for a church service. It took a whole day to get there and a day to get back, but we didn't care."

The kettle was beginning to whistle, and Dixie got up to make two cups of tea. The two of them sat sipping it, and Mrs. Harlow began to talk about those days. She concluded by saying, "I do wish Lars had married. He'd have made someone a wonderful husband."

"Maybe he will yet."

"I don't think so. If he had wanted to marry, he would have done it long before now. He was always very sweet—but the stubbornest man I ever met in my life!"

Mrs. Harlow got up and busied herself setting the table, and Dixie knew she didn't want to talk about Lars Bjoren any longer.

Dixie decided that she would go over and visit Mr. Bjoren and his dogs every day. He took her out with him the first day to watch the training process. "You can watch if you want to. You start out training a lead dog by himself—before you ever hook him up to other dogs. This one's name is Charlie. I don't think he'll do, though. Hasn't got enough drive."

She remembered that he was trying to break in a new lead dog but wasn't having much luck.

"What does he have to do?" Dixie always liked to learn things.

"The main thing a lead dog has to do is keep his tug line taut at all times."

"I read a story once where the lead dog had to turn around and make the other dogs behave."

Lars laughed. "That's just something in a book. It doesn't work that way. A lead dog *never* turns around, and he never fights with other dogs, either! His job is to keep that line tight, and the other dogs learn to follow him. They all have to be tough, but the lead dog will work twice as hard as any other dog in the team."

Every day she learned something new. First, she learned how to harness a dog with a racing harness. The tug line was attached to a point just about the tail base. Then a long guide rope went to it. She watched Mr. Bjoren put on a waist belt. "These dogs can wear you out," he said.

He took along a long pole to tap Charlie if he didn't behave, and then he began teaching the dog.

For two days this went on. The third day, he said, "I can't keep up with Charlie on my old legs," and he brought out a bicycle. Then he proceeded to let Charlie go ahead while he rode behind him.

Dixie saw him teach the dog how to turn right and to turn left. When she asked him about it, he said, "This part is very important. You don't let a dog pick the trail. They have to be trained to go right or left only when the driver says so. The driver's smarter than any dog, no matter what they say."

Dixie was thrilled when he let *her* get on the bicycle and be pulled along by Charlie. And she was pleased when he obeyed her commands "Gee" and "Haw."

After each session with Charlie, they would take a break, and always Dixie would go to Blizzard's pen and spend some time with him.

"Are you ever going to let him be the lead dog?" she asked.

"I'm going to try. He could be the best lead dog in Alaska if he'd just let himself do it. The only thing he doesn't have is a positive attitude."

"Let's try him tomorrow, Mr. Bjoren.

Maybe he'll reform. You've been a good influence on him."

The next day, instead of training Charlie —who got the day off—Lars Bjoren hooked up all the dogs.

Buck whined, wanting to go, and Dixie said, "I'm surprised he'd want to be hooked up. Isn't it work?"

"Good sled dogs want to go, if they're not worked too hard. Buck there, he loves it." Then he brought out Blizzard.

Dixie started over to the dog, but Lars said, "No baby talk, Dixie. That's one thing you don't want to do with a sled dog. It's OK maybe when they're off duty. But once you stand them to harness, it's all business."

Dixie was surprised to see that when Mr. Bjoren put Blizzard in his place, he simply lay down. She did not know what was coming and was shocked when he ran to the dog and grabbed him by the fur on both sides of his head. Holding Blizzard so that he couldn't bite, he shook the dog so hard that Dixie was afraid he'd hurt him. Then he slammed him down again.

"You think that's rough, Dixie, but you have to let them know who's boss. It doesn't really hurt them, and pulling a dog's feet off the ground makes him feel helpless."

"Do you ever whip them?" Dixie asked anxiously.

"Never. Sometimes I slap them on the nose when they get too rambunctious, but that mostly just hurts their feelings. If you have to beat a dog, he's no good."

Almost every night, Dixie and Clarissa and Mrs. Harlow sat around the big stove to read the Bible together and have a prayer time. Before that, they would always talk about their day's activities. Dixie saw that Mrs. Harlow was very interested in everything, so she told her all the details.

"And he has this beautiful dog named Blizzard. He's big. Almost seventy pounds, but he's stubborn."

Mrs. Harlow laughed. "I'd like to know how *that* comes out. A stubborn man and a stubborn dog."

"He's a good trainer," Clarissa said. "Everybody says that."

"He's not sure he'll ever make a lead dog out of Blizzard, though," Dixie said. "He says he'd be the best he ever had— maybe the best there ever was—but he's stubborn. Blizzard is just contrary most of the time. A lead dog is supposed to stand there while the rest of the dogs are being leashed. And keep the line tight. Well, Blizzard will back up and let it go limp. Or he'll just lie down. Or turn sideways. Every time he does it, Mr. Bjoren will just jerk him into place again and say, 'Bad dog!'"

"Well, I hate to say it, but maybe he's getting a dose of his own medicine," Mrs. Harlow said. "*He* would never take advice from anybody, and now he's got a dog that's the same way."

As the training of Blizzard went on, Dixie grew more and more interested. She also grew more and more fond of the beautiful husky. The first thing she did every day was go to see him. She would sit in his pen, and he would lie with his head in her lap while she stroked his fur and talked to him.

More than once, Lars Bjoren stood outside the pen and shook his head in wonderment. "I can't believe that he's letting you do that. He just doesn't seem to like me."

"I think he's getting more gentle," Dixie said. "I sure would like to see him be the lead dog to take Buck's place."

"I'd like to see that, too."

Dixie watched closely and saw that every time Mr. Bjoren tried to teach Blizzard something, he had ways of doing it that were not cruel. But she wondered if his system was working.

When Blizzard sat down when he was supposed to be standing, Lars Bjoren would step on his tail. When he would move too far to one side, Lars would step on his toes. Sometimes he turned sideways when he wasn't supposed to, and the big man would walk right into him, striking him with his knees.

"I know you think this is bad," he explained. "But there can be only one boss with a racing team. And that's the driver, Dixie. The dog's job is to go straight forward at the best possible speed for the conditions. He's got to respond immediately to commands when he's in full stride. If he hesitates, or loafs, or looks back, he'll be run over by the other dogs. So there's got to be a perfect understanding between a dog and the driver."

The days passed quickly, and Dixie kept learning new things about huskies. She was fascinated. While she and Lars

Bjoren were together with Blizzard, she told him many stories about how animal trainers in the circus trained the big cats, and these stories seemed to fascinate *him.*

"I don't see how in the world anybody would *want* to get in a cage with tigers or lions," he said one day. They were sitting in his kitchen, drinking hot chocolate. It had snowed again and was cold outside, so the chocolate tasted good. There was also gingerbread, which Lars had made according to Dixie's training. Dixie secretly thought it was not as good as hers, but she'd bragged on him anyway.

"They start when the lions and tigers are only cubs," she said, "and sometimes they don't let anybody else feed them. I knew one animal trainer that hadn't had a vacation for five years. Every day he feeds his cats."

"Yeah, but just one bad moment and one of those critters could turn around and bite your head off."

"I know," Dixie said. "But they never did while I was with the circus. And Stripes was just like a big kitten. He wouldn't hurt me for anything."

After they had talked for a long time

about the circus, Dixie said, "We're having a special service at church Sunday, Mr. Bjoren. I wish you'd come."

Instantly Lars Bjoren's face changed. "No, I won't be there."

When Dixie told Mrs. Harlow, she said, "That's the way he is, Dixie, and I don't guess he's ever going to change. You can't teach an old dog new tricks."

"Mr. Bjoren's not an old dog! Why, he's no older than you are!"

Martha Harlow laughed. "As a matter of fact, our birthdays are on the same day."

"Really?"

"Yes. We always used to celebrate them together." She looked thoughtful. "I've missed that a lot."

Dixie filed this away for future reference, then said, "And you *can* teach an old dog new tricks. I learned that in the circus. Old animals *can* learn tricks, and I'm going to get Mr. Bjoren to church or else know the reason why."

Dixie's Alaska visit was one-third over. She had been in Bannock for a month, and she'd found it an exciting time indeed. She and Bingo and Debby had become fast friends. She enjoyed the church a great deal and had not missed a service.

But Lars Bjoren and his dogs, especially Blizzard, had become the chief interest in her life. By the end of that first month, to her delight, she was able to hitch up Blizzard and he would stand still at her command. Then she learned how to hitch up the whole team.

Lars Bjoren laughed, saying, "You're probably the youngest race driver in the world!"

"Except that I'm not a driver. I've never driven them."

"No time like the present."

Dixie stared. "You mean I can really drive them today?"

"Sure you can."

She had been out with Mr. Bjoren and the team many times, and she knew the basic commands, Go, Gee, Haw, and Whoa. And with Buck in the lead there should be no problem.

"Don't try to trot along behind them like I do. Ride. That will help keep the sled down," he advised her. "Stand on this thing right here."

Dixie got up on the small board made for the driver's feet. She felt nervous. "What if they don't do what I tell them to?"

"Look at old Buck there. He's ready to go."

The husky's ears were pointed forward. The line was taut.

"All right," she said, then called, "Go!"

Immediately Buck trotted off, and the six other dogs in harness trotted obediently after him. Dixie hung on with both hands, still feeling a bit scared. Then she saw that Lars Bjoren was trotting along behind her, and this gave her more confidence.

When they came to a turn to the left,

she hollered, "Haw, Buck!" and Buck instantly turned left.

"That was good. You timed it just right, Dixie!" Mr. Bjoren called to her.

Dixie drove the dogs for more than an hour, and when she brought them back home again, the big man gave her a hug.

"That was wonderful! I didn't know you had it in you, Dixie."

"It was such fun! Can I do it again sometime? Tomorrow?"

"I don't see why not. Maybe we can even give you a chance to run Blizzard as lead dog."

The next day Dixie hooked Blizzard up with the other dogs, and again Buck whined, begging to be allowed to go.

"Only one lead dog at a time, Buck. Sorry," Dixie called. She looked at Blizzard. He was standing alertly with his ears perked forward. She had never talked baby talk to him once he was hooked up, but she did whisper, "Good dog," and he licked her face.

She got on the sled and yelled, "All right, Blizzard. *Go!*" The dog leaned into the trace, and she whizzed out the driveway.

When they came to the first turn, Dixie

was nervous. She knew that Blizzard had not taken Mr. Bjoren's commands but had gone right past the turns, refusing to obey. "Come on, Blizzard. Do what I tell you," she breathed, then yelled, *"Gee!"* The husky instantly turned right, and the others followed.

"He did it! He did it, Mr. Bjoren!"

"Like a champion!" Lars shouted, trotting along beside the sled. "Keep going! You'll make a lead dog out of that critter yet!"

At supper that night, Dixie spilled her news to Mrs. Harlow and Clarissa. She was telling them about Blizzard and how well he'd done, when she was interrupted by a knock on the door.

"I'll see who that is. You two go on," Clarissa's mother said and left the room.

Dixie heard the door open. She heard a man's voice and then Mrs. Harlow saying, "Why . . . yes. Come in."

"I'll just wait here. Ask her to come out, if you will."

When Clarissa's mother came back, Dixie thought that she seemed agitated and was somewhat pale.

"It's—it's Lars Bjoren. He wants to talk to *you*, Dixie."

"To me?" Dixie got up and headed for the front door.

Mrs. Harlow looked at Clarissa and shook her head. "It gave me such a shock seeing Lars standing there. He vowed he'd never come into this house again."

"Whatever can he want?"

"I don't know. I suppose Dixie will tell us, though."

Soon Dixie came back. "Mr. Bjoren has to make a trip. He asked me to feed his dogs for a few days and take care of them while he's gone. Is it all right?"

"Why, of course. Is there some sort of trouble?"

"He didn't say," Dixie answered. "He just said that he had to be gone."

"That's rather strange. Once in a while he goes off like this on business affairs but never so suddenly. And usually Frank Dakas takes care of his dogs. But Frank's away, so I suppose that's why he asked you, Dixie."

"It's quite a responsibility," Clarissa said.

"I can do it," Dixie said. Then she

added, "I think we need to pray for Mr. Bjoren. He's so unhappy."

The two women exchanged glances, and Mrs. Harlow said quietly, "I've been praying for him for years, but we can all three pray together now."

For the next three days, Dixie practically lived at Lars Bjoren's house. She got there shortly after dawn and stayed most of the day. She returned home when it was nearly dark.

They were eating breakfast on the fourth day, when Clarissa said, "You're going to work yourself to death, Dixie."

Dixie did, indeed, feel tired. But she said, "I'm all right. It's fun. I got the house cleaned up, too. Men aren't very good at housekeeping sometimes."

They were almost through with breakfast when suddenly Dixie lifted her head. "I hear an airplane."

"It has to be Lars," Mrs. Harlow said. "He's got a little landing strip out there. I hope it's not covered with snow."

"Let's go welcome him back," Dixie said, "and I'll give him his house key."

The three of them climbed into the

Land Rover, and Clarissa drove to Lars Bjoren's house. The little plane was just taxiing in as they got there.

"I'll wait in the car," Mrs. Harlow said. "You go on."

Clarissa and Dixie ran toward the plane.

They waited at a safe distance until the engine was shut off and the propeller ceased whirling. Then the door opened, and Lars Bjoren climbed stiffly out. He looked at them, a strange expression on his face.

"Hello, Mr. Bjoren," Dixie said with a smile. "We came to welcome you back. Did you have a good trip?"

Lars lifted his eyes to where Martha Harlow was sitting in the Land Rover over by the house.

He did not answer for so long that Dixie wondered if something bad had happened. "What's wrong? Is it bad news?" Dixie asked.

"I'm afraid it is," he said slowly. "My brother and his wife were killed in an automobile accident last week."

"Oh, I'm so sorry!" Clarissa said. "And he was your only brother."

"Yes. We were very close even though we were separated by many miles."

"I'm sorry, Mr. Bjoren," Dixie said quietly. On impulse, she went to him and took his hand. Looking up into his face, she said, "I hope they knew the Lord."

"They did. They were both fine Christians."

Suddenly a strange sound emerged from the plane. Dixie and Clarissa both stared at Lars, and Dixie said, "Is that a *baby?*"

Lars Bjoren shifted his feet. "My brother and his wife had two children." He turned around and said, "Come on out, Katy."

A small girl appeared at the door of the plane. She had blonde hair and blue eyes very much like her uncle's. She looked tired and as if she had been crying. She was perhaps ten years old.

"Katy, this is Dixie Morris. I hope you two will be great friends. This is Miss Harlow. And this is Katy."

"Hello, Katy," Dixie said at once. She wanted to say she was sorry but thought it might be better to say, "You and I can have a lot of fun together."

"I guess so," Katy said.

Then Lars reached inside the plane and undid some straps. He turned back with a bundle in his arms. "And this is Nathan."

Clarissa and Dixie went close. A baby with big blue eyes stared at them out of the blanket.

"Oh, can I hold him?" Dixie cried.

Mr. Bjoren gave the baby to Dixie and stood watching as she and Clarissa exclaimed over how perfect his skin was. "If you'd take him into the house, I'd appreciate it. I'll carry in the luggage."

When they approached the Land Rover, Mrs. Harlow got out to meet them. She listened while Clarissa briefly explained what had happened, and then she greeted Katy with a kind smile and an invitation to come and visit. When Mr. Bjoren came up with the bags, she said, "I'm so sorry, Lars. I was always very fond of John."

"He liked you, too, Martha," he said gruffly.

"Why don't you let us help get the youngsters settled?" she asked quietly.

Mrs. Harlow and Clarissa and Dixie waited. Dixie expected Lars Bjoren to say no. But Lars Bjoren was a changed man. She saw the new lines of worry in his face and the troubled look in his fine blue eyes.

Finally, he said, almost in a whisper, "That's like you, Martha. I appreciate it."

At once the three hopped into action, and Lars Bjoren had to stand by while his house was overturned. Dixie came up to him once, holding Nathan and saying, "I'll bet he'll be a great sled dog driver when he grows up. You can teach him how. You'll have to be a father to him now. And I'll help you with Katy. She'll need a friend."

"Thanks, Dixie."

Lars Bjoren had struggled with what to do about his young niece and baby nephew. He'd brought them to Alaska, knowing that he was the poorest-fitted man in the world to raise two children. But there was no one else to take care of them. And now as he watched Dixie and Clarissa and Martha Harlow working busily to settle his new charges, Lars Bjoren said a prayer of thanks to his heavenly Father—for the first time in many years.

DIXIE TAKES OVER

Dixie stayed a while after Mrs. Harlow and Clarissa went home. She kept as busy as a one-armed paperhanger. And she soon discovered that Lars Bjoren was almost useless where the children were concerned. As she changed Nathan's diaper, she glanced up to see that the big man was standing helplessly by, watching. It was as if he had never seen a baby changed before. She said, "It's really not hard to change a diaper."

Mr. Bjoren looked down at his big hands. "I'm afraid to pick him up. He's so little, I might hurt him."

Dixie slipped pajamas onto Nathan, who looked up at her and gurgled and grinned a toothless grin.

"See, he's laughing at me! He's such a

good-natured baby—you're not going to have any trouble with him at all."

"That's what you say. And now Katy's feeling sick, and I don't know what to do for her."

"Was she sick before you left?"

"No. She got sick on the airplane."

"Maybe it's just travel sickness then. She'll be all right tomorrow. Just give her an aspirin and let her sleep."

"How many aspirins?" he asked help-lessly.

"Just one."

As Nathan's father obediently trudged off to perform this chore, Dixie warmed some baby food. By the time she was feeding Nathan, his uncle came back, looking sad. "She says she feels awful, and she's crying again. She cried almost all the way here."

"This week has not been easy for her. We'll all have to work hard to make her feel at home here," Dixie said. "Here, open your mouth, Nathan. Eat your peas like a good boy."

Dixie fed the baby another spoonful. Then she said, "Why don't you sit down and feed Nathan, Mr. Bjoren? You might as well get used to it."

Looking almost frightened, the big man sat in the rocking chair and took the baby in his arms.

Dixie moved the baby food jar close to him and watched as he heaped up a big spoonful. "Not that much!" she said. "Just a little bit."

This time he put a tiny fragment on, and she said, "No. More than that."

Feeding a baby was obviously quite a difficult thing for Lars Bjoren to do, but under Dixie's direction he eventually filled Nathan up.

"I think that's about all he wants. He's spitting it out."

"What do we do now?" he asked.

"Why, you burp him—like this—and then you rock him until he goes to sleep. If you want to."

"I don't know a thing about babies."

Dixie had never had a small brother or sister, but she had had experience taking care of the neighbors' baby. She pulled up a chair and watched as he began rocking, holding the baby awkwardly. "He's not going to break," she said.

The big blond man cautiously picked up one tiny hand. "Look at his fingers.

They're just like a real person's, only smaller."

Dixie laughed. "He *is* a real person! He just hasn't grown up yet."

Suddenly Lars Bjoren looked at her and smiled. "I don't know what I would have done without you, Dixie."

"Well, Clarissa and her mother have helped a lot, too. We all want to help. And we're going to."

Lars did not respond to that. Instead, he looked down into the face of the baby. "He looks like my brother, I think. But Katy looks like her mother."

"That's good. Every time you look at them, you'll remember your brother and sister-in-law. I hope there are lots of pictures. You'll want to show them to Nathan as he grows up."

"A whole boxful and lots of home movies."

The house grew silent except for the creaking of the rocking chair. Nathan dropped off to sleep, but Dixie did not offer to take him. *It's better,* she thought, *if Mr. Bjoren handles him as much as possible.*

"What will I do if he gets sick?" Lars Bjoren asked, a worried frown on his face.

"Well, he *might* get colic . . ."

"What's colic?"

"A tummy ache."

"What do you do for it?"

"Mr. Bjoren, you need to buy a book with all this stuff in it, and you need lots of help. We'll all help you." She took a deep breath and decided to take a chance. "But what you most need is the Lord to help you."

"I've left God out of my life, Dixie. Why should He help me now?"

"That's no way to talk. We all fail God. I have—a thousand times. But the Bible says that He loves us, and He wants us to love Him."

"If somebody ignored *me* for twenty years and then came around, I wouldn't want anything to do with him."

"Well, that's not what *God* is like. The story of the prodigal son in the Bible—it says the father was glad to see the boy come home, even after he had been so bad."

Reluctantly he nodded. "That's what the story says all right, but it's hard for me to take it in."

When it was time for Dixie to go home, Lars Bjoren looked apprehensive. "You'll come back tomorrow?"

"First thing in the morning. But I don't

think you'll have any trouble. And Katy ought to be feeling better by then."

She put on her coat and cap and left, thinking, *But he's going to have more problems than he can handle, if he doesn't learn how to let the Lord help him.*

"Dixie said she was going over to help with the children this morning." Clarissa was making pancakes. She turned one over and glanced at her mother, who was sitting at the kitchen table and nursing a cup of coffee. "I've thought about Lars Bjoren and those two children a lot. Couldn't sleep last night."

"Neither could I," Mrs. Harlow said. "His brother and wife—they were such fine people."

"Did you know them well?"

"Not really well. He was young when they left here, but I remember him. He was always full of fun. Just like Lars."

Keeping one eye on the pancake, Clarissa said, "It's hard for me to think of Lars Bjoren as happy-go-lucky. He's always so serious and grumpy."

"I'm probably one of the few who remember him as being that way," her mother replied. She sipped her coffee, and her eyes closed. "He was always so much fun," she repeated.

"More than Daddy?"

"They were a lot alike—and they were the best of friends."

"How in the world is he going to get along with those two little ones?" Clarissa slipped the spatula under the pancake and added it to the stack beneath the cloth she was using to keep them warm. "Dixie!" she called. "Breakfast is ready!"

Dixie came out almost at once, her face glowing and her eyes bright. "Pancakes!" she cried. "My favorite!"

"Everything's your favorite for breakfast," Mrs. Harlow teased. "Now, sit down there and try not to make a pig out of yourself."

"What's the use of having pancakes if you can't be a pig?" Dixie waited until Mrs. Harlow asked the blessing, then took two. "Can I have three?"

"Why not?" Clarissa said.

Between bites, Dixie commented, "That Nathan is the sweetest baby. He's so good."

"Well, that's a fortunate thing," Clarissa said. "Lars Bjoren needs all the help he can get."

"What's going to happen to them?" Dixie asked. "Mr. Bjoren doesn't know the first thing about babies."

Clarissa's mother pushed around a morsel of pancake in the maple syrup on her plate. When she looked up there was a thoughtful look in her eyes. "I've been thinking about it a lot and praying too. Lars is not going to have a very happy life until he's . . . broken."

Clarissa nodded. "I think you're right, Mom. He's very self-reliant, and self-reliant people just aren't very happy. It takes a humble spirit before God."

"And that's what Lars has never had," her mother said. "But he'd better have it, or he's going to have a terrible time."

Lars Bjoren tried everything, but nothing he did seemed to please Katy. He prepared bacon and sausage and eggs and toast for breakfast, but she complained that it wasn't like the breakfasts her mother fixed. Patiently he said, "I'm not as good a cook as your mother, Katy, but this is the best I can do."

She also complained about her clothes. It seems that he had left behind some of her favorite dresses.

"You didn't have anything much for cold weather. We'll have to get you some more," he said.

Katy looked up from her plate and frowned. "I don't want new clothes! I want my old clothes!"

"But you'd freeze to death in them up here, Katy. You don't know how cold it gets. Those summery dresses you had—you couldn't wear them but a few weeks of the year around here!"

"I want them anyway! Mom picked them out for me!"

All morning long, Lars did the best that he could. Finally he lost all his patience and snapped at her. "I know things aren't the way you like them, but we just have to make the best of it!" He was appalled when Katy burst out crying and ran to her room.

"Now look what I've done," he said to Nathan, who was watching him owlishly. "Why don't *you* start on me?"

But Nathan merely flailed his fists and grinned toothlessly.

At that moment a knock came, and Lars went to admit Dixie. "Glad to see you," he said.

"What's the matter, Mr. Bjoren?"

99

"It's Katy. Nothing satisfies her."

Dixie listened as he related how everything displeased the little girl. She said, "Why don't you go take care of the dogs, Mr. Bjoren, and I'll take care of Nathan and Katy?"

"Gladly. And I hope she's nicer to you than she was to me."

As soon as Lars Bjoren left, Dixie went to Katy's door and knocked. "Katy, come on out and talk to me."

The door opened. There was a pouting, mulish expression on Katy's face. "I don't want to stay here. I want to go home."

Dixie smiled and gave her a hug. "Let's do some baking. Do you like to bake?"

"I don't know. I never tried."

"It's fun. We'll make some brownies. I'm pretty good at that. Do you like brownies?"

"Yes. I like brownies a lot."

"Then I'll show you how to make them, and you can make them anytime you want to. For you and your Uncle Lars and Nathan."

"I don't care about making anything for Uncle Lars. He doesn't like me."

"He likes you very much, Katy. Now, let's make those brownies."

Dixie measured a cup of butter into a large pan and added four squares of unsweetened chocolate. She cooked the mix slowly over medium heat, stirring occasionally and waiting patiently until the butter melted. Then she added two cups of sugar, one and one-half cups of flour, four eggs, one teaspoon of salt, one teaspoon of baking soda, and two teaspoons of vanilla. She was glad to see Katy take an interest in the process.

Dixie let her stir the mixture with a wooden spoon for about four minutes, and then gently she folded a cup of chocolate chips into the brownie batter. She greased a baking pan, poured in the batter, and placed the pan in the oven.

While the brownies were baking, Dixie was as cheerful as she knew how to be. "Tomorrow's Sunday," she said. "We'll go to church. You'll like that. There are some kids there I want you to meet."

"I don't want to meet anybody!"

"Oh, you'll like these kids!" She talked about the boys and girls that Katy would meet at Sunday school. Afterward she said,

"As soon as the brownies are done, I'll hook up Blizzard to the little sled, and you can ride. That'll be fun, won't it?"

"I guess."

Her uncle came in shortly, and Dixie told him, "Mr. Bjoren, Katy and I want to go for a sled ride. Could I hook up Blizzard to the little sled, and will you take care of Nathan?"

"Sure. That'll be fine. Would you like that, Katy?"

"I guess."

"Come on, then," Dixie said. "Get some heavy clothes on. It's cold out there."

Fifteen minutes later, Katy was sitting in the sled, and Dixie was trotting along behind. She called out commands to Blizzard, and he obeyed her without hesitation.

By the time they got back from a long ride, Katy's cheeks were rosy. "That was fun," she admitted. "Do you suppose I could learn to drive?"

"Sure. I'd never driven in my life till I came here. Your Uncle Lars will be glad to teach you. He's good at this."

All day long Dixie stayed with Lars Bjoren and the children. He went out to work with the dogs once in a while, but much of the time he stayed inside, saying little and watching Dixie a lot.

When it was time for her to go home, he said, "You're a wonder, Dixie. I wish you could stay here all the time."

"Why don't you play games or something with Katy tonight?" she suggested. "She's still lonesome and unhappy, and she needs lots of love and attention."

"I'll do that."

"And tomorrow is Sunday. I wish you'd all come to church with us."

"Katy can go, but I don't think I will."

Dixie did not coax, but she said quickly, "All right. We'll be along in the Land Rover to get her about ten o'clock. Let Nathan go, too. There's a baby nursery."

Dixie went home and reported the results of her day.

Mrs. Harlow said, "That's good, Dixie. Katy needs some friends."

"And so does Lars," Dixie said.

Mrs. Harlow met her glance with a smile. "God's going to give him a friend. I think we can count on that. My prayers and your prayers—God is sure to answer them."

Dixie went to bed, looking forward to the next day.

FRIENDS FOR KATY

Clarissa stopped the big Land Rover in front of Lars Bjoren's home. Her mother had gone on to church early in her Toyota. Dixie said, "I'll run in and get them."

It had snowed two or three inches during the night, and Dixie enjoyed making tracks in the fresh snow. It was like a shining white carpet. When she knocked, the door opened almost at once.

"Hi, Mr. Bjoren," she said. "Are Katy and Nathan ready to go?"

"Yes. But are you sure you want to do this?"

"Sure. I love church, and they will, too." She looked around him and saw Katy. She was standing back, looking somewhat afraid. "Hi, Katy. We're all going to Bingo's house after church and play games."

"Who'll take care of Nathan?" Katy asked.

"Oh, the babies have a special room where they play. They'll be glad to take care of a fine boy like this."

Nathan was crawling around on the floor, already dressed in his snowsuit. She picked him up with a grunt. "You come with me, Nathan. You're going to have a fine time today with all the other little boys and girls."

As they went out, Dixie said, "Don't worry, Mr. Bjoren. We'll bring them back after we have our little party at Bingo's."

Lars Bjoren followed them out to the Land Rover. "This seems like a lot of trouble for you, Clarissa."

"No trouble at all. Just wish you'd go with us."

"Maybe sometime."

Clarissa nodded cheerfully and waved as they started off. "We'll see you later."

When they got to church, Clarissa said, "Let me take Nathan to the nursery. You take Katy with you."

Katy was hanging back, but Dixie said, "Come and meet the Sunday school kids. It's not quite time to start yet."

She took her into a small metal building next to the church. It had been divided into four rooms. There she found some of her Alaska friends, laughing and talking.

"This is Katy Bjoren," she said. "She's my new friend, and she's going to be yours too. Katy, this is Bingo, and this is Debby Sturgis . . ." She went around the room, naming all the youngsters.

At that moment Miss Stags, their teacher, came in. Dixie introduced her visitor, and Miss Stags said warmly, "We're always glad to have a new member in the class. You girls get out of your coats now. We've got a good story this morning."

Katy sat close to Dixie and seemed to listen attentively. Miss Stags used lots of stories and threw in a joke now and then. Dixie thought the lesson part was very good indeed.

After the bell rang, they all walked over to the church building for the preaching. "Let's all sit together on one bench," Dixie said.

"I want to sit by you, Dixie," Katy said quickly.

"Sure. You sit here, and I'll sit right beside you."

"How about if I sit in your lap?" Bingo said. "This bench is pretty crowded." His eyes twinkled, and he started to sit on her.

She punched him and said, "Go sit on a tack, Bingo!"

After church, Dixie introduced Katy to Pastor Henderson.

"I'm glad to see you in church, young lady. I'll come by to visit you later on in the week. Tell your uncle I'll be coming."

Then Clarissa drove Dixie and Katy and Nathan to Bingo's house. The other kids from Sunday school were there, too. Mr. Bingley cooked hamburgers on the grill until he finally protested, "You kids are going to founder!"

"No, we won't, Dad," Bingo said. "Just keep 'em coming."

Afterward they went into the Bingley rec room where Bingo's parents had collected many kinds of games. There was even a Ping-Pong table.

It turned out that Katy was very good at Ping-Pong. She was able to beat everyone except Bingo.

Bingo bragged on her considerably, saying, "You're my buddy, Katy. Anybody who can come that close to beating me has to be all right."

Katy seemed to enjoy her time at the Bingleys'. But on the way home, she said, "I wish I didn't have to go back to Uncle Lars's house."

"Why, Katy!" Clarissa said, steering carefully in the fresh snow. "You and Nathan are going to have a fine home with your Uncle Lars."

Later, Dixie and Clarissa told Mrs. Harlow about the fun afternoon at the Bingleys' house. But then Clarissa said, "I don't like the looks of things, though. I think Katy's *afraid* of Lars."

After supper, Martha Harlow said, "I'm going out for a drive. Will you two take care of the dishes?"

She got into the Toyota and drove straight to Lars Bjoren's house. She felt a little odd, for he had not invited her. Still, there were things she had to say to him.

She parked at the front door, got out, took a deep breath, and knocked firmly. The door opened, and she said, "Hello, Lars. I need to talk to you."

Lars Bjoren looked shocked. But he

stepped back and said, rather reluctantly, "Come on in. Is something wrong?"

Martha waited until he had closed the door, then she asked, "Where is Katy?"

"Already gone to bed. Why? Did you want to see her?"

"No, I want to see you."

Lars stared at her. "Well, come on in to the fire." He stepped aside and followed her.

She glanced around, noting that the house was neat. "You don't do bad house-keeping for a man," she said with a smile.

He did not answer that remark. "What's wrong? You've never come here in all the years I've lived here."

"You never invited me."

"Well, you never invited me, either!"

"Yes, I did. When you first came. You ignored me."

Lars shifted his weight from one foot to the other. "Well, what do you want to talk to me about?"

"About Katy. I'm worried about her."

"I'm worried about her, too. Nothing pleases her. I start out being nice and easy, and the first thing I know I'm yelling at her."

"And that's just what you mustn't do,

Lars," Martha said. "You've got to be gentle. You know about dogs, but you don't know anything about little girls."

"How could I? I've never been around any."

"I know," she said quickly, "but you've got to learn."

"Do you want to sit down?"

"Yes. It looks like we might have a long talk."

"Then I'll make some coffee. Do you still drink coffee?"

"Yes."

"With cream and two spoonfuls of sugar?"

"I'm surprised you remember after all these years."

"I remember a lot of things."

He trudged off, and Martha Harlow sat quietly before the fire until he came back with two large mugs on a tray. She took hers, tasted the coffee, and said, "You still use too much coffee."

"It suits me." Lars sipped his and seemed to be waiting for her to start talking. When she did not, he said, "I want you to know how much I appreciate what you've all done."

"It's been mostly Dixie."

"She's been a real soldier, and she's so good with Katy."

"Lars, I haven't had a chance to tell you how much I grieve over the loss of your brother. I'm so sorry."

"I miss him every day."

For nearly an hour Martha sat in Lars Bjoren's house. Lars would not say much, but from time to time he looked at her in an odd way that brought warmth to her face. "I just wanted to come over and assure you that we all want to help with Katy and Nathan," she said.

When Martha Harlow left, Lars Bjoren stood at the door, watching the Toyota disappear into the darkness. Then he turned about and stood dead still in the center of the room. "Lord," he said aloud, "You know I need help with these kids. Somehow I've got to make it, but I don't know how."

For the next two weeks, Dixie divided her time between learning more about Siberian huskies and taking care of Nathan. The time seemed to fly by.

Although she was not able to get Lars Bjoren to go to church, he seemed to grow more appreciative of her every day. And he lavished on her his teaching concerning how to train a good leader for a dog team.

While Katy was playing with Nathan one afternoon, Dixie and Mr. Bjoren hitched up the team. Dixie listened as he lectured her.

He put Minnie, the last dog, in harness and said, "Let me give you a breakdown on how to *ruin* a good dog. First thing you can do is to get in front of him. The lead dog should *always* be in front. At no time ever allow a person or another dog or *anything* to get in front of him. Another way to ruin a good dog is to haul him around by his collar. Never pull a leader around by his collar. It won't hurt to do that with other dogs, but never the leader."

"I never do, Mr. Bjoren."

"Good. Another way to ruin a good dog is by asking too much of him. You've got to remember, Dixie, that lead dogs work harder than the others, and it's an easy thing to get upset with a dog doing what he can't help."

"What do you mean?"

"I've seen a time when the whole team backed up. The leader was trying to go forward, but he got dragged backward. And the driver went up and cuffed the leader for something he couldn't help."

"That's awful!"

"Yes, it is. Then, you also don't want to try to make the leader do *everything*. Especially don't insist that he be the best puller. His job's hard enough as it is. Let the others do the work, and let him keep them on line. Well, that's enough for this lecture. Get on," he said, "and I'll let you drive this time."

Dixie got behind the sled at first and started the dogs by hollering, "Go!"

As always, she felt a sense of excitement when Blizzard jumped forward and the others followed him. The sled runners hissed on top of the snow, and she ran along behind them for a while. She could not run as far as Mr. Bjoren, of course, and, since her weight was nothing to the team, she rode most of the time.

This time Lars said, "Let them go full speed, Dixie!"

She cried, "Faster!" and immediately Blizzard picked up the pace. The dogs were running at top speed out the gate when she saw a turn coming up. She knew it was hard and that Blizzard would run right by it if she didn't call the right command at exactly the right time. She waited until he was less than five feet away, then yelled, "Haw, Blizzard! Haw!"

Instantly the dog turned left, and she heard Lars calling as he trotted along behind. "That's great! Just right!"

When they arrived back at the house, she unhitched the dogs by herself and helped put the harness away. It had been a fine run for the dogs, who seemed to enjoy it, and for Dixie, too.

"You going to enter the race for youngsters at the Pioneer Days celebration?"

Dixie knew about the celebration that Bannock had once a year. People came from all over and competed for all sorts of prizes. The dog sled races were among the most popular contests. She looked at him in surprise. "I never thought of it!"

"You really ought to. The youngsters go up to age sixteen, though, so you'd have lots of competition."

"Would you really let me use your team?"

"Why not? I won't be entering anything."

Dixie hurried home and at once told Mrs. Harlow. "There's a prize. I don't know how much, but Mr. Bjoren said it was money. I could use that to spend in Africa when I get there."

"You sure could. Although," Clarissa's mother said, "it's not likely you'll win. The boys and girls around here have been driving teams for a long time. Others come from hundreds of miles just for the celebration. But you ought to try it anyway."

"I think I will," Dixie said.

Dixie began practicing every day. Mr. Bjoren even took her to where the race would be held, and they went over the track until she knew it perfectly.

The only thing that wasn't going well was the matter of Lars Bjoren and Katy. No matter how hard he tried, it seemed they just couldn't get along. The truth was, as Mrs. Harlow wisely said, that Katy was probably a little spoiled and he was almost totally ignorant of little girls.

It all blew up one Tuesday afternoon. Dixie was outside pulling Nathan on a small sled. She had him wedged in, and he was laughing as she towed him along. When she got back to the house, she saw the Toyota parked in front.

Dixie picked up Nathan and started to go in. She was surprised to hear angry voices. As she stepped inside and shut the door, she realized that Martha Harlow was having an argument with Lars Bjoren.

"It's none of your *business*, Martha!" she heard him say angrily.

"It's my business when you don't take proper care of these children!"

"Who says I'm not taking proper care of them? I see that they get plenty to eat, and they've got a roof over their heads!"

Martha's voice was cold as polar ice. "There's more to taking care of children than feeding them, Lars Bjoren! I should think even you would have sense enough to know that!"

When he began to bluster, Mrs. Harlow said with disgust, "You're acting like a child!"

And then Dixie—who wondered where Katy was during all of this—heard Mr. Bjoren yell, "If you had married me, I would have been different!"

There was a moment of silence, and then Clarissa's mother said in a strained voice, "We went over that years ago. I felt it was God's will for George and me to marry, but you never could accept that. You've wasted the best years of your life just sulking, Lars! And that's so sad."

Dixie could not hear a sound then. She wondered what in the world was happening. Tiptoeing to the end of the short hall that led to the living area, she peered around the corner.

Lars Bjoren was just standing in front

of Mrs. Harlow. He had an odd expression on his face. Dixie didn't know whether he was angry or what, but his face was pale.

Then she heard him say, "Well, I'm sorry that I've behaved so badly, but I just couldn't take it when you married George. I still love you, Martha. To this very day."

Dixie backed down the hall with Nathan, carefully opened the door, and went outside. At the same time she heard the back door slam and knew that someone had gone out. She rounded the house and found Katy standing on the back step. She was trembling. At once Dixie knew the girl had heard what had been said.

"I'm afraid," Katy said. "I don't know what's going to happen to me."

"Don't you worry," Dixie said, holding Nathan close and putting her free arm around the smaller girl. "You just have to be patient with your Uncle Lars. He doesn't understand little girls yet—like Mrs. Harlow says. But when Lars Bjoren comes back to God, he's going to be great! You just wait and see!"

10
KID ON A SLED

The little town of Bannock was as packed as a can of sardines. People had come from all over the area. They filled the small motel. Others had managed to find rooms with residents. Many of them camped out. A small village of tents had been thrown up just east of town. Pioneer Days lasted for two days.

Dixie was enjoying the events tremendously. She kept Katy with her, and at every chance she said something positive to her about her new home and her new family.

"Your uncle wants to be like a dad to you," she said once.

"He could never take my dad's place!"

"No, nobody could do that, but he can be *another* dad to you," Dixie said. They were walking along the main street, which was lined with concession stands. Dixie said, "Let's stop and get a hot dog. I'm hungry."

"All right."

The boy behind the counter asked, "What'll it be?"

"Two big fat hot dogs with lots of mustard, chowchow, and chili."

"Coming right up!" He quickly produced two masterpieces. "Come back if these don't fill you up." He grinned, taking the money from Dixie's hand.

"What time is your race?" Katy asked, biting off one end of her hot dog. "Ouch, that's hot!"

Dixie was just nibbling at her own hot dog. She suddenly discovered that she had butterflies in her stomach and was not hungry after all. "Two o'clock. That's an hour from now."

"Are you scared?"

"I'm not scared," she said, then added. "I'm a little bit *nervous,* I guess."

"I bet you win," Katy said. "I hope so, anyway."

"Everybody says there's not much chance for that, but it'll be fun to try."

"Everybody says Uncle Lars's team is the best."

"It probably is. Now that he's got Blizzard as his lead dog, I think that if he were driving, he could beat anybody. I bet he wins the Iditarod this year. I wish I could be here to see that, but I'll be in Africa by then."

"If you've got the best team, you'll win."

"There's more to driving than the dogs. The driver's got to be smart, too."

"Well, you're smart. And I'm going to pray you'll do your best."

Dixie was glad to hear Katy talk like that. She reached over and hugged her. "That'll be good," she said.

The two consumed their hot dogs as they wandered on down the street, but Dixie could think only of the race. She said, "It's a little early, but I've got to go and get ready."

"I'm going to go find Bingo and stand with him."

"OK. I hope I come in the winner. I'll wave at you if I do, Katy."

All across the field, teenagers and boys and girls were nervously waiting for the starting signal.

Mr. Bjoren had not tried to give Dixie

125

any more instructions. "You know enough to win right now, Dixie. These are smart dogs, especially Blizzard. You just tell them what to do, and they'll bring you home a winner."

"Why don't you go stand beside Katy and watch the race, Mr. Bjoren?"

He suddenly grinned. "I guess I'd better. And I'll be right there when you bring the winner home."

Then the signal sounded.

"Go, Blizzard! Go!"

Blizzard lunged forward. All the dogs behind him threw their weight against the harness.

As Lars Bjoren's team shot along, Dixie soon saw that only three other teams were ahead of her. They all crossed a broad field and soon came to a trail that was plainly marked by yellow streamers.

What Dixie feared most was that she would collide with another team, get all tangled up, and never have a chance. When another team drove straight toward her, she said, "Slow down, Blizzard!" The dogs all heard her slow down signal and let the other team go on.

The driver was a redheaded girl who

laughed at Dixie as she swept by. She was older than Dixie, probably close to sixteen, and had a team of all black dogs.

"I'll pass you! You just wait and see!" Dixie called to her.

That's the team to beat, she thought, gritting her teeth. "Faster, Blizzard!" she yelled, and the team picked up speed again.

It was a difficult race. She knew that from time to time somebody would fall by the wayside. In fact, two of the teams ahead got entangled, as Dixie had feared she might, but she stayed in the clear. Lars Bjoren's dogs ran beautifully, obeying her every command.

When they started the last lap, she glanced back and saw that only she and the red-haired girl were in the running. Dixie gauged the distance and realized that if she was going to win, she would have to pass the black team quickly. She knew there was only one more spot where teams could pass, and she urged the dogs to a greater speed.

Turning a corner with them, she saw the level passing spot and knew that this was the only chance she'd have. *"Faster, Blizzard!"* she yelled, and at once the dogs picked up their pace.

The trail was narrow, and Mr. Bjoren had told her that one trouble that most dog teams had was passing other sleds. When Dixie saw that Blizzard's nose was about ten yards behind the girl with the red hair, she called out, "Haw, Blizzard!"

The big dog lunged to his left. The others followed.

Dixie's dogs were pulling up fast. Then she was even with the red-haired girl, who gave her a furious look.

"I'll beat you, yet!" the redhead yelled.

"Go, Blizzard!" Dixie shouted.

Dixie glanced over at her competitor and saw that the girl had gotten the best out of her dogs. But she believed there was still more strength in Lars Bjoren's team, so she called out, "Come on, Blizzard! You can do it, boy! *Faster!*"

She felt the dogs' extra burst of speed, and slowly they pulled away, passing the black huskies one pair at a time. When she was safely past the lead black dog, she called, "Gee!" and Blizzard immediately swung to his right.

And that was the way they came down the main street—Blizzard and his team pulling for all they were worth, Dixie yelling, and the red-haired girl with the black dogs twenty yards behind.

As Dixie passed under the finish line, she caught a glimpse of people she knew. She saw Bingo, practically turning back flips. She saw Debby Sturgis screaming. She saw Mrs. Harlow and Clarissa clapping. Then she flashed by Lars Bjoren. He had Katy sitting on his shoulder, and she was waving and yelling, "Dixie!" Dixie waved back.

And then the race was over.

Mr. Bjoren ran up and hugged her. "You did great!" he said. "Just great!"

Dixie took everyone's congratulations and then went straight to the red-haired girl. "You drove a great race," she said. "You've got a great team there."

The redhead grinned ruefully. "Thanks. Didn't have quite enough today. Maybe next year."

"I'll be in Africa next year, but I hope you win."

Martha Harlow stood at the finish line, watching all of this. Then she went up to Lars Bjoren, who now was standing alone.

"Lars," she said, "there's something you ought to do."

"What's that, Martha?"

"You ought to enter the Kid on a Sled."

"But that's a race for fathers and their sons or daughters."

"And that's what you are. It would make Katy feel real good if you'd do it with her."

"Martha, I can't keep up with these young fellas."

Martha Harlow looked at him very sternly. "Lars Bjoren, I think you still can do just about anything you set your mind to. Now you go enter Kid on a Sled, and you win for Katy—and for me!" she added.

Suddenly he laughed. "All right, Martha. I'll feel like a fool, but I'll do it."

"Where's Katy?" Dixie asked Mrs. Harlow.

"Over there. See her on that sled?"

"What kind of a contest is this?"

"It's for fathers and their children. See? Each father puts his youngster on a sled, and there's a race. The dads are the dog teams. They do all the pulling."

"I bet you talked Mr. Bjoren into that, didn't you?"

"I sure did. And look at Katy. I've never seen her so excited. She was so pleased when he asked her about the two of them entering the race."

Dixie watched the Kid on a Sled racers get ready. The contestants all lined up, and she noticed that almost all the fathers were younger than Lars Bjoren. But there he was anyway, looking rather sheepish.

"I'm so proud of him," Dixie said.

"I am, too," Mrs. Harlow murmured. "It was a sweet thing to do, even if I had to think of it for him. Lars is a good man. He just doesn't think of things like this."

"I bet he would if you were around to prod him," Dixie said.

There was a sudden gunshot, and somebody yelled, "They're off!"

The crowd lined both sides of the race track. It was short—only a hundred yards long—but the snow was deep. The going was hard, and Mr. Bjoren fell behind at first.

Dixie's heart sank. "Oh, I wish he'd win!" she cried.

"He will. I've known him all of my life, and Lars Bjoren never quit on anything. There—he's gaining now."

Only three dads and sleds were ahead of Lars now. Katy was yelling. Lars was leaning forward into the harness. Then he began to yell, too.

He passed one contestant, then another. The third father, he stayed even with.

"Come on, Mr. Bjoren! Come on, Lars!" Dixie screamed.

And Lars Bjoren pulled past, winning the race by a full five yards.

"We did it, Dad! We did it!" Katy yelled.

As Dixie and Clarissa and her mother closed in on them, Dixie saw tears in the big man's eyes.

Lars Bjoren picked up Katy from the sled. "Did you hear what you just called me?"

"No. What?"

"You called me Dad."

Katy looked at him for a moment. "I'm sorry. I didn't know what I was saying."

"Don't be sorry," he said quickly. He kissed her on the cheek. "I hope that one of these days you'll be calling me that all the time. You had the best dad in the world, but I'm going to do the best I can to be number two."

When Martha Harlow turned away, there were tears in *her* eyes.

Dixie smiled. *Things are going to be just great,* she thought. *Thank You, Lord.*

When Lars Bjoren walked into church, every eye in the place turned and stared at him. He came in late—the song service was just ending—and the choir, led by Phineas Bean today, got a little more off-key than usual.

Dixie was shocked. She had gone with Clarissa to pick up Katy and Nathan, as usual. She had said, also as usual, "I wish you'd come with us, Mr. Bjoren." But he had said nothing at all, and she had turned and gotten into the Toyota.

The big man paused and let his eyes run over the congregation. Dixie saw him spot her, sitting beside Katy, and he made his way to their bench. He leaned over and said, "Could you make room for an old man?"

"Sure," Katy said. "You can sit between us."

He sat down and winked at Dixie then. "You never expected to see me, did you?"

"I knew you'd come sometime. I just didn't know what day," Dixie answered.

The pastor had some difficulty getting the attention of his congregation. Everyone knew the history of Lars Bjoren and Martha Harlow. And now they were sitting on the same bench, though not side by side.

Pastor Lewis Henderson was a wise man. In his sermon he emphasized the love of God. He preached a short message today, but it was one of the finest sermons that Dixie had ever heard. From time to time, she secretly glanced upward and saw that Mr. Bjoren was listening intently.

At the close of his sermon, the preacher said, "I'm going to give an invitation this morning, and if any of you want to come forward to make known your faith in Christ—or with any other decision—I shall be glad to pray with you."

The choir sang, and Dixie hoped that Mr. Bjoren would go forward, but he did not.

He did, however, turn to Dixie after the

last song and say, "That was a fine sermon." He was very serious, too.

When the preacher shook his hand, he said very little except, "I appreciated the message."

On the way home from church, Dixie listened to Clarissa and her mother talk about Mr. Bjoren's unexpected visit.

"I nearly fell over," Clarissa said, "when he came through the door. I'd given up on him."

"I hadn't." Mrs. Harlow's voice was firm, and there was a small smile on her lips.

"You really expected him to come?"

"Sooner or later. I knew that God was dealing with him."

"Well, I wish he had gone forward or made some sort of move."

"He will," her mother said. "Just give him time."

After lunch the next day, Dixie went to play with Katy and help with Nathan. She'd decided to say nothing to Mr. Bjoren about his visit to church.

He seemed glad to see her, and after they had visited the dogs, he asked, "I wonder if you would mind staying with Katy until I get back."

"Oh, sure! Where are you going, Mr. Bjoren?"

"I thought I'd go hunting. Mostly I just need to get away where it's quiet for a while."

"Why, sure. Stay as long as you want to. I told them at home I might be late."

"Thanks." He smiled at her, then began preparing to go.

Back inside the house, Dixie heard the engine of his snowmobile cranking up. Going to the window, she said, "Your dad said he's going hunting."

Katy watched the snowmobile take off, throwing a plume of snow behind it. "He said he's going to take me someday."

"You two have really gotten to be good friends since Pioneer Days, haven't you?"

"We sure have, and I was so excited when he came to church yesterday. Did you know he reads the Bible every day now? Sometimes he reads it out loud to me."

The afternoon passed so quickly that Dixie was surprised when she looked out and saw that it was actually getting dark.

They had been playing Monopoly, and she'd forgotten the time.

"Why, look what time it is!" she said. "It's almost dark!"

Katy looked a little worried. "I wonder where Dad is."

"I thought he'd be back before now," Dixie said. "He'll be here soon, I'm sure."

But Lars Bjoren did not come back soon. Minutes passed, and then an hour, then darkness fell. And Dixie said, "I think something might be wrong, Katy."

Katy gave her a frightened look. "Do you think something's happened to him?"

"I think maybe the engine quit on his snowmobile, and he couldn't get back. I think I'd better get home and tell Mrs. Harlow. She'll want to send somebody out to look for him."

"I'm afraid to stay here by myself."

"Why don't you go with me, then? We can take turns carrying Nathan."

Dixie put a note on the door for Mr. Bjoren, telling him where they were in case he came back. Then they left the house. It was a long walk for Katy, and by the time they got to the Harlows' store, she was tired.

"Mrs. Harlow," Dixie said right away, "I'm afraid Mr. Bjoren had some kind of engine trouble on his snowmobile."

"He went somewhere on it?"

"He went out hunting about noon, and he still hasn't come back. I thought we ought to go looking for him in the car."

"That wouldn't do much good if he was hunting on a snowmobile," Clarissa said. "We'll get some of the men who have snowmobiles to go out looking."

At once her mother jumped into action on the telephone. She called every snowmobile owner she could think of and told them to come to the store. There they would divide up and search in different directions.

Dixie was still hopeful Lars Bjoren would come for them at the store. However, he did not come, and she knew that something must be very wrong. She began to pray, "Lord, don't let anything happen to him. Take care of him, and don't let him be hurt."

12

A VOICE BEHIND HER

That night, Dixie lay awake for a long time thinking about Lars Bjoren. She actually never did go sound asleep, and at the first hint of activity in the kitchen she jumped up and ran out of her room. She found Mrs. Harlow making coffee. "Did they find him?"

The woman's face looked tired as she shook her head. "Not yet. We've got at least twenty men out on snowmobiles, still looking, but no sign of him yet."

"Couldn't they follow his tracks?"

"Could have if it hadn't snowed right after he left. Just enough to cover them up."

"I forgot about that," Dixie said.

"Clarissa's in the store. Why don't you help me with breakfast?" Mrs. Harlow asked.

"Then we'll spend some time praying for Lars."

After breakfast and a time of prayer for Lars Bjoren, Dixie said, "I'm going to go feed his dogs. I know they're hungry."

"If he does happen to come home, be sure to tell us at once. I'm so worried about him."

Dixie made the trip on the double. The fresh snow was soft and fluffy under her feet. Ordinarily, she would have taken pleasure in making footprints in the new snowfall. But today, all she could think of was Mr. Bjoren out somewhere, perhaps hurt and unable to help himself.

She fed the dogs, then went in to sit beside Blizzard as she often did. As she ran her hand over his fur, he nuzzled her. She said, "Mr. Bjoren said it's not good to talk baby talk to the lead dog, but I don't think it'll hurt unless you're in harness."

Blizzard seemed to grin. He snuggled against her so that she would stroke his head some more.

Dixie sat with the husky for a long time, just stroking him. She began to pray out loud. "Lord, help me to trust You. We've all prayed for Mr. Bjoren, but if there's anything *I* can do to get him home, I'd be glad to do it."

She sat a while longer after praying this prayer, and then a Bible verse popped into her mind. Mrs. Harlow had been reading through the book of Isaiah, and they had reached the thirtieth chapter just two days ago. Dixie had been so impressed with verse twenty-one that she'd memorized it. And now it came back to her: *Your ears will hear a word behind you, "This is the way, walk in it," whenever you turn to the right or to the left.*

She sat thinking about that verse. She sighed. *I sure wish I could hear a voice behind me telling me how to get to where Mr. Bjoren is. Where would he go to hunt?* She sat still a little longer, then suddenly she said out loud, "I remember the day he took me to that place over behind the hills—that little valley. He said nobody knew about it but him—and that it was a good hunting place."

Excitedly, she jumped to her feet. "I wonder if he went *there.* He said he wanted a quiet place, so maybe he did. And nobody would ever think of looking there!"

She thought of running back to tell

Mrs. Harlow, but then another thought came. *All the men are already out looking. If he's hurt, he may need help real quick.* She looked down at Blizzard.

"Maybe the Lord is telling me that you and I and the rest of the team ought to go and see if Mr. Bjoren is out there, hurt. We'll do it, Blizzard!"

It was the first time that Dixie had ever hitched the team to the sled without Lars Bjoren watching her, but she did it without a problem. Blizzard stood stock-still while she slipped the harness on him, and he held the line tight while she did the next two dogs. Soon she had the other dogs ready. Then she ran to the back of the sled. "All right, Blizzard. *Go!*"

Blizzard leaped forward, followed by the rest of the team. The sled runners hissed over the new snow, which plumed up behind them. Dixie was not exactly sure how to get to the secret valley, and she began to pray, "Lord, I need Your voice behind me now. Help me make the right turns."

For a time there was no problem, but then she came to a fork in the road. There was no time to think. She just breathed a prayer, said, "Gee!" and watched the dogs veer to the right. It went like that for a long time.

But at last Dixie cried out, "There it is! There's the hill! That secret valley's right behind it!" She guided the team through the narrow trail between the trees and toward the hill.

Dixie emerged in the valley and stopped the huskies. She was disappointed, for there was no sign of a snowmobile. Slowly she said, "I guess I was wrong." Just to be sure, she shouted, "Mr. Bjoren—Lars!"

It was silent in the valley except for the shuffling and panting of the dogs. She was almost ready to start back when she thought she heard a sound. She left the team, knowing that Blizzard would keep the other dogs still, and ran toward where it seemed the sound had come from. "Lars, where are you?"

"Over here!" The voice was so faint she could hardly hear it.

Dixie turned quickly and ran toward it. She was about to call out again when she burst into an open area. There stood the snowmobile—and there was Lars Bjoren, pinned down by a big branch.

Dixie ran to him. "Mr. Bjoren, are you all right?"

"What are you doing here?" he whispered. His lips were blue with the cold, but his eyes were clear.

"I came looking for you. I thought of this place. Everybody's out looking, but they'd never think of looking here. What happened?"

"I was going to pull this dead limb down to get some firewood, and the whole thing collapsed right on top of me. I can't move it off."

Dixie studied the log. It had a natural crook in it, and it bent over his legs.

"If it had been straight, it would have broken my legs. The snow was a cushion, but I just can't get out."

Dixie tugged at the limb but soon realized that was useless.

"It's too heavy for you, Dixie. You'll have to go back and get help."

And then she had an idea. "The dogs can pull it off."

"They might do it," he murmured. "If you could maneuver the sled in here, you could tie on, and maybe just one tug will roll it over."

"I'll go get the team."

Five minutes later, Dixie had the sled positioned. Mr. Bjoren was propped up on his elbows, telling her how to fasten the nylon rope he always carried. She tied one end around the limb and the other to the back of the sled.

"I still don't know if they can do this or not. It's pretty heavy," he said.

"They can do it," Dixie said confidently. She went back and took her position on the sled, then she cried, "Blizzard, *go!*"

The dogs all lurched forward. Their feet threw snow, but the log did not move.

"Faster, Blizzard! Faster!" Dixie yelled.

At first the limb did not move at all. Then it shifted just a fraction.

"You're doing it! Go on, Blizzard! Faster!"

And then the dogs seemed to gain traction. They lunged ahead, the limb moved, and Lars Bjoren pulled himself out.

"All free!" he called.

Dixie cried, "Whoa!" and then ran back to him. "Are your legs all right?"

"Well, they're numb." He flexed them. "But not broken," he said with relief.

"Let's see if we can get you to the sled."

It took some doing. Lars Bjoren's legs were so numb that he could barely crawl. But finally, with a thump, he rolled over onto the sled. Dixie wrapped a blanket around him. Then she grinned. "Now I'm the boss!"

"You sure are, Dixie. I don't see how you ever knew I'd be here."

Dixie thought for a moment and then smiled again. "Well, I heard a voice behind me saying, 'This is the way, walk in it.'"

"*Whose* voice?"

"I think it must have been the Lord's. Nobody else knew you were here."

The big man laughed and reached up to hug her. "I wouldn't have believed that a little while ago, but I do now." He released her, saying, "Take us home, Dixie. You and Blizzard."

Dixie looked over at Lars Bjoren. He was seated beside the fireplace in Mrs. Harlow's house. She had brought him straight here, and the two women half carried him inside. Then Dixie put up the dogs in a shed for the night and came back to find him telling his story.

"And here's the heroine," he said.

"Come here, Dixie, and give an old man a hug."

Dixie did, then sat in a chair and listened as he continued.

"Some of you may have noticed that in church the Lord has been putting things on me pretty hard."

"I saw that," Martha Harlow said softly.

"Well, I decided to go out alone and think and pray. But I pulled that stupid limb down on myself. And then, of course, there wasn't anything to do *but* pray. So I prayed—at first not even to get out from under that limb but that I'd find my way back to God."

"And did you, Lars?" Martha Harlow asked quietly.

Lars Bjoren looked at her. "Yes, I did, and I'll never leave Him again. He's been good to keep me these years. And now He's given me a family to take care of. I'm going to follow Him." Again he looked over at Dixie. "I was interested in hearing how He guided you to me, Dixie. I'm going to need lots of guidance from Him in the days to come."

Dixie smiled happily. She looked at Katy, who was seated as close as she could get to her new father. She looked at Nathan, who was cuddled in Mrs. Harlow's arms, and she knew it would be all right. "I think the Lord speaks to us when we are ready to listen," Clarissa's mother said. "You just weren't ready to really listen until you were under that limb."

"That's right." He looked over at Nathan and then squeezed Katy. "I'm going to teach you kids to listen to God before a limb falls on you."

Martha Harlow laughed at that. But she got up and walked over to him and put her free hand on his shoulder. "I'm glad you're back with the Lord, Lars. I've missed you." She leaned over and kissed him on the cheek, then turned and left the room.

Dixie winked at Katy. She thought she knew a secret.

13

A QUIET GAME OF SCRABBLE

The one game that Dixie played with Katy that involved no shouting or loud screaming or noise whatsoever was Scrabble.

Dixie discovered that they both had skill at making words, but it was a game that required much concentration. They had set a time limit of three minutes to think of each word, and in that time no one was allowed to speak.

They were playing in Dixie's room, and it was her turn. She'd been staring at the board for approximately two minutes in total silence. Once she looked up to see Katy grinning at her, because Katy was ahead.

She looked at the timer and saw that her three minutes were almost up. The timer was an hourglass, and the sand was almost all emptied into the lower part.

Dixie had just reached out to place a letter when the front door opened.

Lars Bjoren's voice said, "I know you're busy, but I've got to talk to you."

Katy put her finger to her lips and mouthed the words, "Be quiet."

Dixie didn't know what to do, for she didn't like to eavesdrop. But Katy's eyes were sparkling, and it was good to see her so happy.

Then she heard Mr. Bjoren say, "Martha, quite a few years ago in this very parlor I asked you to marry me, and you told me no. Do you remember that night?"

"Of course, I remember it."

"Well, I'm not going to beat around the bush. You know I haven't been following God for all these years, but I'm back now. And what I want to know is, will you give me a second chance? I want to marry you, Martha. I want us to raise these kids—they need a dad *and* a mom."

Both Dixie and Katy were as still as statues waiting for Martha's reply. When she said, "Yes. I will marry you, Lars," Katy jumped up and let out a scream.

Dixie leaped to her feet, too, and followed as Katy ran into the living room and threw herself into Mrs. Harlow's arms.

"I'm glad you're going to be my mom," Katy said.

"Were you eavesdropping?" Mr. Bjoren asked.

"I was, Dad—and if she had said no, I was going to come in and argue for you."

After they all calmed down, Mrs. Harlow said, "You're going to have to court me a little bit more than this, Lars Bjoren."

"I'll get my guitar and come and sing to you," he agreed happily. "I'll write stupid love poems, and I'll send you candy and flowers every day."

"Wow, that'll be fun!" Dixie said.

Lars leaned over and kissed her. "Dixie, you and Blizzard saved my life the other night. You've also been a big help in putting this family together."

Dixie grinned. "Always glad to oblige. Dixie Morris Matrimonial Service. We never close."

It was almost dusk, and the sky was crimson in the west. Dixie had been spending some time with Lars Bjoren's dogs. Sitting beside Blizzard now, she stroked his head absently. As always, the dog looked as if he was grinning at her.

"Blizzard," she said, "in just a month I'll have to leave. I'll be with my mom and my dad in Africa."

Blizzard said, "Woof!" and licked her face.

Dixie grabbed him and shook him roughly. "I'll miss you, Blizzard, but it would be too hot for you to live in Africa. Besides, you've got to stay here and take care of your new family."

She stood up, and the big dog stood with her. She looked out over the snow-covered plain to the mountains rising far off in the distance. Then she looked again at the husky. "But I'm going to miss you, Blizzard," she said again.

The big dog looked up at her and said, "Woof!"

Kneeling, Dixie threw her arms around him and buried her face in his fur. "I hope there are dogs in heaven, Blizzard, because I'd like to go on a heavenly sled ride with you!"

Blizzard said, "Woof."

With a laugh and bark, Dixie and Blizzard began to run through the snow. "There won't be much snow in Africa, Blizzard—but God will have some cool animals for me to make friends with!"